BUCKLETT'S
PURSUIT

BUCKLETT'S PURSUIT

A Western Novel

JIM WORKMAN

authorHOUSE®

AuthorHouse™
1663 Liberty Drive
Bloomington, IN 47403
www.authorhouse.com
Phone: 1-800-839-8640

Published by AuthorHouse   01/18/2013

ISBN: 978-1-4817-0589-9 (sc)
ISBN: 978-1-4817-0588-2 (hc)
ISBN: 978-1-4817-0587-5 (e)

Library of Congress Control Number: 2013900446

Any people depicted in stock imagery provided by Thinkstock are models, and such images are being used for illustrative purposes only.
Certain stock imagery © Thinkstock.

This book is printed on acid-free paper.

This Book is dedicated to the memory
Of my beloved wife
Joyce Marlene Workman
for her inspiration and motivation

PROLOGUE

A light mist began to fall from moisture-laden clouds, obscuring the surrounding mountain-tops and promising more of the heavy rain which had inundated the valley in recent weeks.

In the valley below, two wide-shouldered men stood beside an open grave on a fog-shrouded knoll. Before them a plain wooden casket had been fashioned from weathered boards, which the two brothers had stripped from the family cabin.

Earth and stone striking the casket disturbed the early morning calm. The men continued their somber chore in dismal silence. After erecting a simple hand-carved cross, the two joined a third man standing slightly apart.

"I'm sorry; I would have gotten here a little sooner if it had been possible. I want you to know that," Doctor Letmer said apologetically as they trudged toward the cabin. "But with so many creeks and rivers running out of hands, I'm damn lucky to get to any of my patients."

Will Bucklett made a clearing sound in his throat. "We appreciate you coming out anyway, Doc. You did all you could for Ma; we couldn't have asked you to do more. We're obliged to you."

"She was a vigorous woman, your mother was. A body can only take so much, no matter how strong they are," Doctor Letmer said. "Sometimes a grieving heart can be as disastrous as the illness which she was unable to overcome."

"Ya mean Pa?" Dain Bucklett asked, as they neared the log cabin.

"Yeah, son, I mean your pa. Why he went out west leaving your ma back here all alone, I'll never understand. I don't see why he couldn't have waited until you boys had return from that stupid, senseless war before he took off."

"I guess Pa had his reasons," Dain quipped defensively.

"Oh, I know. We've heard of the talk and rumors about many the fantastic opportunities out west, but still . . ." Letmer broke off. "You men got any plans now?"

The three men had now arrived at the cabin. A home that had once been full of warmth, joy and laughter, now appeared dejected and forlorn, as though already abandoned.

"Not much to hold us around here," Will said, with a wave of his hand. "I figure to see if we can find out what happened to Pa. According to a letter he had written to Ma, he should have been home weeks ago. We were hoping he would show. Ma had her heart set on him being home 'for she'd taken ill."

Dain's head was lowered as he spoke. "Seems like Ma just lost heart and all hope when Pa didn't come home, almost like she thought something had happened to him." The sadness lingered in his eyes as he lifted them to meet the gaze of Doctor Letmer. "Pa had his faults like all men, but he never lied to Ma. If he made a promised to her he wouldn't break it, come hell or high water. Something happened or he would have been here as he promised Ma."

Doctor Letmer nodded his head in understanding. "So, you're going to look for him. What about the place here?"

Will gave a shrug and said, "Not much here worth a lot. There's a little hay in the barn and a fair stand of corn in the bottoms. Think you could see to it that some of the folks around here could share in it?" He paused, looking toward the cabin that no longer felt like home. He thought of the things that had been used, and loved by his mother. He knew she would have wanted them put to good use. She had never approved of waste. "Maybe you could also see that things like the old rocking chair, spinning wheel, churn and other house goods could get into hands that could care for them as Ma did. We'll be traveling light, and will have no other need for such."

"Be glad to," the doctor complied. "Folks will appreciate that," he reached to shake each brother's hand in turn, he said. "Well, I'd best be on my way. Mrs. Wheeles is due to deliver any day now, and Horace Dunlap had a sick calf. Not much telling how many more folks is out looking for me now."

Doctor Letmer turned toward his horse, stopped short and pointed up the mountain. "What the hell is that?" He suddenly asked.

Will and Dain followed his gaze. Through the heavy, misty fog there appeared a wraith-like form, standing over their mother's grave. A robe or cloak was draped over the individual's shoulders. His arms were out stretched high over his head. Soft, rhythmic chanting floated forebodingly over the valley floor.

"Booger Red," Dain volunteered. "That's his way of showing respect."

"Thought that old half-breed would be dead by now," Doctor Letmer quipped. "Wonder where he's been keeping himself?"

Handing the doctor his medical bag, Will said, "No one seems to know. He appears and disappears like a ghost. But he always seems to be near when there's a need."

ONE

The three men urged the weary mounts forward, topping a rise to survey the clapboarded town below. A river flowing beside the town was a welcome sight. Both men and beasts had been pushing relentlessly since leaving the Red River Crossing. Wind, dust and tumbleweeds had been constant companions to the dry, dusty travelers.

Will glanced at the two men beside him. It felt right to be in their company, right and good. It would have never occurred to him to put voice to these thoughts, nor was it necessary. He knew without being told that both Dain and Booger Red held him in the same regard.

Will tugged at the ties holding his battered Confederate Cavalry hat. He brought his forearm across his face, only managing to displace the coating of dust. "Is that Tascosa, Booger Red?" He asked.

"Huh, that it," Booger Red managed to say against the strong wind. He remembered the frontier town from some years back when he had accompanied Salas Bucklett on one of his trips out west.

"Think Pa might still be here, Will?" Dain asked with hope in his voice.

"Don't know," Will answered. "Let's go find out. Besides, if we don't get these horses to water soon, we may find our backsides meeting some tumbleweed."

Slowly, they clucked the horses forward. As they approached town, the pace of the horses quickened with the animals' instinct that water, food, and rest awaited them.

Unpainted, clapboard building lined the single dust-swirling street. By the time they pulled up in front of the livery stable at the edge of town, a few windows began emitting a soft, orange glow. Somewhere, a well pulley strained under a rhythmic squeak. A dog yapped, the sound dying in the quiet solitude. A few cow ponies stood hip-shot at the hitching rail in front of the town's only saloon.

Opening one of the double doors of the stable, Dain gave a hello for the hostler. A short, wiry stubble of an old cow puncher came limping from the interior of the barn.

"Been drawing water for the trough out back. Saw ya'll on the ridge-line up there. Figure ya'd want to wash the dust out of ya craw." He gave them a quizzical look. "It'll be four bits a hoss; all the oats, hay, and water them can hold. Two bits a man to bunk in the loft. Water in the trough out back so ya can wash up, ya wants more ya'll draw it yourself. Ya'll pay in advance." He thrust out a weathered old punchers palm.

Dain counted out some money for the old man. "There's some extra there for rubbing them down. They've come a good ways and are a mite wore down."

Slightly offended, the old man scowled, "They'll get no better treatment in the great state of Texas. I know good hoss flesh when I see it. I ain't blind. And I'll tell ya another thing: don't even think about calling me Limpy. Name's Shorty. I've been known to take offense at anything else. Last man to call me Limpy had to unbuckle his belt from around his neck for a long time to come."

Shorty's audience looked at him in silence. Each was willing to take him at his word. The wiry strength they saw was there in spite of age. His life of hard work held him in good stead. He would not be a man to be dismissed lightly if riled.

"Okay, Shorty. No problem here," Will said, suppressing a grin. "Now, would you mind going to the trouble of pointing out where we might get a bite of grub?"

"Bess's Café is the best there is between Abilene and Santa Fe. She lies on a feed bag heavy for a cowpoke. She's just up the street on the other side," he pointed out. "She'll welcome you, too." He paused with a small gleam in his eyes. "But you can't go there."

"Why is that?" Will asked?

"She's closed. Closes at sundown, but she'll be open early for breakfast. And she got grits, biscuits and such." Shorty raised his eyebrows. "If you want to eat tonight, you'll have to get it at the saloon. The beef could be a mite tough at times, but the beans are good. Mexican beans, they is."

"Might not want to go there though," he nodded toward Booger Red. "Some folks ain't too partial to Indians around here. Especially since Black Kettle's young bucks been raising hell, raiding and stealin' horses over in the Nations. Those heathens were a-murdering women, kidnapping young'uns and all. Damn sure raising cane since Chivington massacred that bunch up at Sand Creek."

"Booger Red is our friend. Where we go, he goes," Will stated. "It's as simple as that."

"Your problem," Shorty shrugged.

The wind had lost very little of its strength as the three men pushed open the weathered double doors to the saloon. A dust-laden strong, gust slapped the door out of Will's hand and slammed it against the wall. Gritty dust and wind filled the saloon; playing cards went flying around the room as well as a few hats.

"Shut the darn door," someone yelled. "Where the hell was you born, in a damn barn?"

Men scrambled to pick up their cards and hats which had blown to the floor, while the other occupants turned to stare angrily at the annoying intruders.

"Howdy folks," Will said by way of an apology. "Didn't mean to barge in on you boys unannounced, so to speak, but Shorty down at the livery stable was saying how a traveler might get a decent meal and something to wash the dust on down a man's gullet?"

Will really didn't expect a friendly response, nor did he receive any answer to his greeting. However, the tension seemed to ease somewhat, and after a few moments mumbling conversation returned to near normal. Still, the three drew a few curious scowls as they seated themselves at one of the empty plank tables.

Will lowered his six-foot plus frame onto a cane bottom straight back, which groaned under his solid, rock-hard frame, he suddenly became aware the rickety chair threaten to collapse with any excess movement. The table, assembled from rough hewn timbers, also wobbled shockingly as they seated themselves.

The bartender wiped his short, stubby hands on an apron hanging from his thick waist as he approached their table. His walk resembled nothing less than a constipated duck. The expression on his face revealed a like nature.

"We don't allow Indians to stinks up the place," he sneered. Swinging his beady eyes around the table, they came to rest on Booger Red. "He'll have to go outside."

Dain lifted his head. His ice blue eyes penetrated the bartender's massive bulk, causing him to step back from the table.

"Barkeep, from the smell of this place, I bet I could move a whole Cheyenne tribe in here complete with horses, dogs and the like, and it would be a hell of a great improvement," Dain said frigidly.

Will, knowing his brother was building a head full of stream, decided to interrupt. "I'm sure you would like to keep your establishment, such as it is, in its present state of repair," Will stated. "I'll be right friendly and give you some advice. It would be downright foolish for you to refuse to feed us," Will continued as though he were explaining to a child. "It's our upbringing to be real sociable, except when we're hungry, of course. Then our dispositions could be compared to an irritated razorback hog. Truthfully, we're mighty hungry right now. We've been hungry ever since we left Arkansas. You might want to see that we have a pot of hot, black coffee, and three cups while we're waiting for those steak and beans. And I'm sure, you being a reasonable person; you won't keep us waiting too long for our food."

There was a flurry of snickers and light laughter as the scowling bartender went to the stove and returned with coffee and cups.

"You were going to ask about Pa?" Dain asked impatiently.

"Take it easy," Will answer, looking around the room. "There is a time and place for everything. Most folks like to hear themselves talk, especially without being asked."

Each of the coal oil wall lamps hanging on the walls gave off a soft, orange glow. Occupied tables and chairs were scattered throughout the room. Toward the rear of the room five men sat at one of the tables. Two of the men were no doubt storekeepers. The others were obviously cowhands, with wide-brimmed, sweat-stained hats, thorn-scarred chaps and much faded shirts and vest long overdue for the washtub. A fifth man, straddling a straight back chair with his back to the wall, kept glancing toward Will's table. Will couldn't help but notice the Union Blue Cavalry hat pulled low over his eyes. Will had no doubt he was taking note of Will's Confederate clothes. Probably can't let the war die, Will thought. Most people wanted to forget, but there were still a few diehards that couldn't let go for one reason or another.

Shorty came into the saloon just as the bartender placed three heaping plates of food before the three hungry men. Shorty gave a nod in greeting and went on to the bar.

The steaks might have been a little tough as Shorty had said, but they were so hungry they didn't notice. The beans were hot, hot, and hotter. Will was sure his teeth were going to fall out since the beans were burning away his gums. Dain was certain his nose hairs were burning and would never grow back. Booger Red, more accustomed to fiery food, thought they were damn good; yep, damn good.

The card game suddenly broke up and the two cowhands ambled over to the bar. They were talking to Shorty, in what sounded like a disagreement over something or other, when the front door flew open. Dust and wind again filled the saloon.

The newcomer slammed the doors with a few choice words of vicious frustration. He glanced around the saloon, his gaze lingering momentarily on Will, Dain and Booger Red. He stepped up to the bar, and was soon joined by the man wearing the Union Cavalry hat. Will immediately noticed that men both were sporting tied down holsters.

The bartender sat drinks before them, and they began speaking in low tones, occasionally throwing sidewise glances toward Will and his partners. They were leaving little doubt who they were discussing. The last thing Will wanted was trouble.

Booger Red finished his meal, gave a healthy burp and stated he was going to spread his blankets in the loft at the livery after checking their horses. Will and Dain moved up to the bar and ordered whiskey. The barkeep reached under the bar and brought forth a half-filled bottle of amber liquid. He blew the dust out of a couple of glasses, set them on the bar and turned back to the far end of the bar.

All heads turned toward the door as another man entered with a blast of cold wind. Quickly closing the door, he said, "Howdy, boys. Gonna be frost on the pumpkin in the morning. It's getting down right frigid out tonight." Backing up to the potbellied stove, he glanced around the room and along the bar. His eyes lingered more than a moment on the two men at the end of the bar, and came to rest on Will and Dain. He didn't miss the Henry rifle which Dain had placed on the bar.

"You men strangers in town?" he asked, but his tone was more of a statement than a question.

Will noticing the badge on the man's chest, said, "That depends; I've known this gent beside me for quite a spell. We're slightly acquainted with Shorty here, and we paid our particular howdy to the friendly barkeep, although, I didn't catch his name." Will turned his back to the bar giving the man a level look. "We don't look for trouble, but we don't shuck around it either."

"Well now," he began his voice amiable. "That's a right pretty speech, and if you stick with it, we'll get along just fine. My name's Langley; I'm the city marshal here. Run a quiet town, and want not trouble of any kind from anyone. If there is, they answer to me." He paused for a moment, rubbing his backside. "Hey, Pete," he called, "give me some of that creek water you call whiskey. I've got my rear end thawed; now I'd like to warm my gut."

"We're not looking for trouble," Dain stated. "We're looking for a man."

Suddenly, without exception, all conversation came to a stop. Dain had the undivided attention of everyone in the saloon.

"We're looking for our pa, Salas Bucklett," Dain explained. "I'm Dain Bucklett and this big fellow's my brother, Will Bucklett. We've come a far piece from the hill country of Arkansas to find him. We're thinking; in fact we're pretty sure, Pa was here sometime back. We're hoping we might have some luck picking up his trail here in Tascosa."

"Don't recall anyone by that name," Langley said. "How about you, Shorty?"

Shorty shook his head.

"What about any of you other men?" Langley asked, looking around the room.

"Can't say as I have," one of the cowhands answered, shaking his head. "You, Hank?" he asked, looking at his partner.

"Nope, not unless he looks' like a cow's butt. That's all I've seen. Even see 'em in my dreams." Hank muttered.

"It would most likely be about a month or so back," Will inform them. "A tall, slim fellow, about our size, carries a scar on the right side of his chin, sort of graying at the temples, packs a walrus mustache."

"Say, Marshal," Shorty began, snapping his fingers. "You remember about three to four weeks ago? There was that bunch which same riding in here with the highfalutin' woman? She rode sidesaddle and looked like she just stepped out of a storybook. You remember, don't ya, Marshal?"

"They were only riding through and just stopping for supplies," the marshal recalled. "They rode on out to the north. They were only here for a few hours."

"Something funny about that bunch anyway," Shorty murmured.

"How was that?" Will asked.

"Let's see, as I recall, there were four which rode in, but there were five of them which rode out of town," Shorty answered. "There were three men and then that there lady woman. They separated; one gent and the woman went to Spred's store where they most likely supplied up. The man rode ramrod straight and wore a fancy, black flock coat. I talked to Spred later and he was telling me that there female was one fine lady. But mighty cold, so much so icicles would have dropped off her nose in a summer rain storm. He was saying the gent was a right touchy bastard, giving orders like he was use to having them followed with no questions asked."

"What was so all fired funny about that, Shorty?" Will asked, getting impatient.

"Well, it seemed a little bit peculiar to me," Shorty continued. "Those other two men, seedy looking pokes, they was, sort of stayed out of sight down behind the stables by the old barnyard, which burned down a while back. They didn't go to the saloon, café or in anywhere else, as I recollect. Then when the man and woman left Spred's they rode right straight out of town, due north." Shorty's hands waved this way and that as he continued to explain. "Couple of minutes later, here goes the other two rangy hombres riding like the devil was prodding their coattails. Only now, there were three riders. One of them was a leading the third mans horse, and I couldn't swear to it, but I do believe his partner had a six-gun in his paw. They were moving out mighty fast, so I didn't get a good gander at the tall man's face, but he sat tall in the saddle. His hair might have been graying somewhat. He did have bushy whiskers, best I could tell."

There was silence for a minute as Shorty took a long swig of his beer.

"You never mentioned all this to me, Shorty," the marshal said, as though he felt short-changed.

"Well, no shot were fired," Shorty said in defense. "Didn't seem all that important to me at the time."

Snyder, one of the ranch hands who had been listening intently, said, "I wouldn't want to put you boys on the wrong trail, but some weeks back the boss sent me in to pick up the mail. While I was visiting in Spred's, there was a man there who you might be looking for. Best I can recollect, he sounds like your man. Don't mean to get your hopes up, but the description fits like a glove."

"How long ago did you say that was?" Will turned to Snyder.

"Right after the big sandstorm we had through here which tried to blow New Mexico over to the Kansas Territory, whenever that was," Snyder said.

"That'd be about three, four week, or so ago," volunteered Langley.

"Time matches," Dain concluded.

The sound of coins falling to the bar broke the conversation. The two strangers at the far end of the bar were leaving. Will and Dain studied the two men carefully until the door closed behind them.

Langley noticed Will's interest in the two, and said, "You might want to watch those two hombres. Unless I miss my guess, they're pure poison. They've been hanging around town for some time now. They've been camping down on the Canadian. Ain't done nothing wrong yet, so I got no cause to run 'em out of town, but I'm keeping my eyes on them. They say they're waiting to join up with a trail herd that's supposed to be coming up. But I ain't heard of drive being rounded up, and I'd of most likely got the word by now. But a drive this time of year it being so late? I really doubt it. They could be up to no good."

"As long as they tend to their own business and stay out of our way," Dain said. "But we shy around no man."

No longer interested in the two departed men, Will asked. "Where could we find this man Spred?"

Jake Quigley, sitting at a table close to the bar, answered, "More than likely he's home in bed. He was feeling poorly and closed early. He left the keys with me. If you need supplies, I'll be happy to oblige. I expect he'll be back in his store in the morning."

"Thanks," Will answer. "We don't need supplies tonight. Last thing I want to do is bother a sick man. We'll talk to him tomorrow."

Conversation became general as weather, range conditions, grasslands, various trail drives, and drovers finished out the evening discussion. The brothers gave their thanks for the information, and decided to join Booger Red for some much needed sleep and rest. The air was crisp as they stepped out into the clear, west Texas night. The wind had died down and the stars shone brightly. Preoccupied with the information they had learned of the elder Bucklett, they failed to notice the movement in the dark shadows across the street.

Will's body was silhouetted in the doorway; Dain, ahead of him, had already stepped out and to the side. Will twisted violently, feeling as if his left shoulder had been hit by a ten-pound sledge hammer. He was slammed back hard against the door jamb. Will immediately recognized the report, and knew he had been hit by a large caliber rifle bullet. There was no instant pain, but from experience, he knew the excruciating pain would come later. Dizziness came over him; he wasn't sure if it because his head hitting the door jamb, or because he was shot.

Dain had caught the first muzzle flash out of the corner of his eye. His .44 Remington revolver was in his hand faster than it took to draw another breath. Instinct directing him, he fanned four quick shots. The sound was one of rolling flashes of thunder.

The window above Dain's head shattered as more shots rang out from the darkened alleyway between the buildings across the street.

The deafening sounds of the gunshots died away, leaving an ear ringing silence.

Marshal Langley, Shorty and the other men emerged from the now darkened saloon, guns drawn and ready.

Above the general store, and up and down the street lamps were lit throwing a dim, ghostly glow across the group.

"Put out those dang lights!" cried Langley.

Kneeling beside Will, Dain ordered, "Someone run over and get the doc." Then Dain continued. "Stay with him Marshal, I'll be right back." Then he disappeared into the darkness.

"What the hell happened?" Before anyone could reply, Langley continued, "Damn it all to hell and back. Everything's peaceful around here for months on end, then you three shows up and all hell breaks loose."

Marshal Langley glared at Will. "I've got a good mind to run you all out of town."

Will sat up, his back leaning against the saloon wall. "It seems to me I'm the injured party."

Dain emerged out of the darkness, Booger Red beside him.

Dain squatted beside Will. "Where are you hit, Will?"

"It caught me in the fleshy part of the shoulder. Went straight through, but it hurts like all billy-hell. Any sign of the low life which done the shooting?"

"They done high-tailed it," Dain informed him. "I winged one of them. There's some fresh blood splotches on one of the building over there," Dain nodded across the street.

"How many were there?" Inquired Langley

"Two," Booger Red responded.

The doctor arrived, bag in hand. He was a plump-cheeked, middle-aged man with thinning gray hair. His pants had been quickly pulled up over his night-shirt. Despite his appearance, he had a no-nonsense attitude as he issued orders.

"Get this man inside the saloon where I can take a look at him. And get me some clean, hot water," as an afterthought, he added, "then bring me a bottle of the best whiskey and some hot black coffee."

"Who gets which, Doc?" Will asked.

"I think you need the whiskey more than I do right now," the doctor informed him. "But you'll owe me when this is over."

Marshal Langley pulled Dain to the side as he started to follow Will inside the saloon.

"All right, Bucklett. I want to know the real reason you've come to Tascosa," He demanded. "A man wouldn't get shot just because he's trying to catch up with his old man. What's it all about?"

"We told you the truth of it, Marshal," Dain said, impatient to join Will and the doc. "The last word we had from Pa was sent from right here in Tascosa. He finished what he come up here to do. He was to head home after finishing up a few loose ends."

"What did he come out west for?"

"That we don't know for sure," Dain answered, not wanting to go into detail with what little they knew.

Dain turned and left Langley shaking his head, not satisfied with unanswered questions.

Dain arrived at Will's side to hear the doctor say, "You must be living right. Bullet went clean through, no muscle damage. Going to be painful as all dickens for a week or so, but you'll live." The doctor finished dressing the wound. He swigged down the drink Will had bought for him, accepted the money pressed into his hand and made his farewells.

Having downed a few drinks while the doctor was busy, Will was feeling considerably less pain.

"If you're finished with us, Langley, we could use a little sleep," Will said.

Langley started to agree, but then realized that two people he had expected to see were no longer there.

"Where are Shorty and that half-breed friend of yours?"

Dain answered, "Booger Red made a deal with Shorty for a fresh horse, he'll pick up the trail of those polecats and follow where they lead him."

Snyder spoke up, "He can't track nobody as dark as it is tonight."

"I wouldn't bet any cow chips on that if I was you," said Dain. "Red can track a mosquito through a blinding snow blizzard in the dead of night if he's a mind to. And tell you how much he weighs and how fast he's traveling. Don't put anything past that Injun."

"I figured those two weren't waiting around to join up with no trail herd. I should have run them out of town a long time ago. They must have been hanging around to way-lay you men. But the question is why?" Langley muttered curiously.

"Did you get their names, Marshal?" Will asked.

"One called himself Bo Walker. The other went by the handle of George Getchens," Langley answered. "But I wouldn't put a lot of stock in either one, but least ways that's what they told me. There's no wanted poster on either one of them. I check all strangers passing through; just as I'll be checking out the three of you, hombres. You'd better be telling me the right of it."

Will looked him square in the eye. "We've got no reason to try pulling the wool over your eyes, Marshal."

Langley held Will's gaze for a long moment. Satisfied the he was in the presence of a man with real integrity, he nodded. "All right, I'll accept your word on that. I'll see you both in the morning. Don't leave without me knowing about it."

TWO

Will and Dain rolled out long before dawn, which was their custom. Watering the horses, Will became aware of the gauntness of his sorrel compared to those which Shorty had in his corral. Dain's bay was none the better. The two discussed their need of fresher, well-rested mounts with a much better staying power than what they had ridden out of the Arkansas hills. They needed to be prepared for any type of terrain and circumstance that happen to come their way. Will left Dain to make the necessary arrangements with the liveryman, for fresh mounts. Meanwhile he would call on the general store proprietor before meeting Dain at Bess's Café.

Will found the store was still lock. As he turned from the mercantile locked doors, Marshall Langley was pulling the door closed to his office next door. "Not open yet, huh? Spred must have been feeling mighty poorly yesterday. But he's sure to be in later. Never known him not to open no matter how sick or ailing he was."

Langley stepped off the planked boardwalk. "I was just heading over to the café for some breakfast. Care to join me?"

Without speaking, Will fell in beside Langley crossing the dusty street.

Unwilling to let the silence continue, Langley asked, "How's the shoulder this morning?"

"Tolerable," Will said grimly.

"Where's your brother?"

"Doing a little horse trading with Shorty," Will said. "Ours are a might done in. Figured we better improve somewhat over what we rode in. He's got some pretty good stuff in the corral behind the stables."

Langley laughed. "Smart move."

His laughter drew a questioning look from Will.

"I mean getting better mounts; ones that are more acclimated to the high, dry country," explained the marshal. Chuckling, he continued. "That Shorty! Watch out for that old squint-eyed skin-flint. He's a shrewd one when it comes to horseflesh dealing, he is. Oh, you'll get no better stock this side of the Mississippi. But you'll pay top price, and they'll be stayers. And you can be sure you'll get your money's worth."

Will and the marshal reached the café just as Dain came up riding a wide-chested roan and leading the blazed-face gelding Will had had his eyes on. Dain muttered something about being "dumber than salt lick" when it came to horse trading, as he pull his chair up to the rickety breakfast table.

The rattling of pots and pans came from the kitchen among the high-pitched voice of someone trying in vain to sing the *Rose of Alabama.*

"That's Bess," explained Langley. "She puts out mighty good food if you can stand to hear her crowing."

"You just keep your yap shut, Sam Langley," Bess yelled from the back. "You ain't got room to talk. You kept the whole town up half the night with all the ruckus and shooting going on. Besides, you ain't heard no better singing since your mama sung you to sleep with lullabies, and you know it. So you just watch what you say or I'll cook your steak so tough you'll have to take it to the blacksmith shop to get it broke into bite-size pieces."

Floorboards squeaked under the strain of her massive weight as she came toward them with coffee and mugs. It was an easily discernible fact that here was a female that thoroughly enjoyed her own cooking. Dain guessed her weight to be about two pounds under a ton. Smiling from ear to ear, she asked, "What'll it be, eggs and steak or steak and eggs, cooked or raw?"

Without waiting for an answer, she returned to the rear of the café. She emerged shortly with a huge platter of eggs, three larges steaks, a bowl of grits, and a large pan of steaming biscuits. She made a return trip to the rear and came back with the crowning touch, fresh churned butter and apple butter they could hardly wait to dig into. She surely did know how to make a man's mouth water.

The men ate their breakfast in silence. Conversation would come after the meal, as was the custom of the range. From childhood most were disciplined to never speak with food in their mouth; being taught that with your elbows on the table, and food in your mouth was very ill mannered, and impolite.

"Here's Spred now," the marshal observed. As a rather slim, gaunt man entered the café, he said, "Come on over and have a seat, Spred. Couple of fellows I want you to meet. You look like death warmed over; you sure you feeling okay?"

"Must have been something I ate. I'm as empty as a water bucket with the bottom cut out," he said, lowering himself gingerly in the chair. He glanced around to make sure Bess wasn't within hearing distance. "I made so many trips to the outhouse last night; I wouldn't be surprised if the path isn't a good bit deeper this morning."

Bess greeted Spred with the warmest of smiles setting a platter of steaming food before him. He attacked his meal as if he'd never been a sick day in his life.

Pushing back his cleaned plate, he looked at the marshal. "Some of the boys mentioned you wanted to see me."

Marshal Langley introduced Will and Dain explaining their purpose for being in Tascosa.

Briefly, he told him the information Shorty, Snyder and some of the others supplied concerning the missing Salas Bucklett.

Will described his father to Spred and told him that the last word they received from the senior Bucklett came from Tascosa. It was believed that somehow, Bucklett's travel toward home abruptly come to a stop here in Tascosa for some reason or other. This is where the trail either end or begins; that is the questions that needs to be answered. Will said, "Sure be obliged if you could tell us what you know, if anything. It could possibly be mighty helpful."

"Yeah, I remember the man," Spred began. "It was your father alright, Salas Bucklett. He said his wife's name was Amy. That's who the letter was sent to."

"Was! She passed away some times back," Dain informed him.

"Sorry to hear that," Spred acknowledged. "Bucklett seemed like a likable fellow, someone a fellow could depend on. Said he had been up to the high country, and he was on his way home to fetch the family pretty soon.

"First time he came in was for some supplies; stocked up on bacon, coffee and beans, flour, salt and such. He left and I figured he was heading back east, but a couple of days later he was back in the store. He wanted to borrow a pencil and paper. Started penning him a letter right there on my counter.

"Asked me to see it got off to Arkansas. I made mention if he was going to Arkansas, he would more than likely get there before the letter did. That's when he told me something unexpected come up, and he was going to be delayed for a while."

"Did he say why he was going to be delayed?" Ask Dain.

"No, didn't say. Just he had to take care of some unfinished business. He was acting some different than when he first came into the store. Not as friendly as before; sort of acting like he was maybe—you know, preoccupied, or was studying awfully hard about something. But it sure wasn't the Bucklett which first came into the store, nowhere near as talkative."

Spred arched an eyebrow, "But I believe it had something to do with that lady Shorty was telling you all about."

"Why do you say that?" Ask Will abruptly.

"I guess it was about an hour after he left the store, I saw Salas and the lady in what appeared to be a heated argument down the street by the barber shop. Later that afternoon she came into the store with another fellow. She was dressed real proper like, and full of smug arrogance. And him, well I've never seen such an uppity gent. He tried to order me around like one of his soldier boys."

"You mean they were army people?" Dain asked.

"Didn't see any uniform, if that's what you're asking. However, the way he strutted around, I'll bet my store against a three-legged pup he's been in the army some. Be my guess, a high ranking officer of some sort."

"When they came in was Bucklett with them?" Langley wanted to know.

"No, Sam, they were alone. There was just the two on them."

"Did he come back again? You talk to him anymore?"

"Who's that Sam?"

"Bucklett, damn it."

"Don't get your bowels in an uproar, Sam. No, last I seen, he was riding out with two men I had never seen before. I don't know who they were."

"Who?" Asked Langley.

"Bucklett, damn it."

"Was the woman and her friend with them?" Dain wanted to know.

"No, all I saw was just the two of 'em, and a couple of hard cases and Bucklett."

"Did it look like Bucklett was trying to get away from them?" Langley asked.

"Not that I could see," Spred answered.

Will leaned back in his chair, stretching his long-legged frame. "Can you describe any of these two riders with our pa?"

"Didn't get a good look at the two what rode out with Bucklett, but the woman . . . ." Spred paused, sighing; a wicked smile crossed his face. "She is one homesome lady. About forty-five, I'd guess, raven black hair, fair skin and icy, cold dark eyes. Those piercing dark eyes fairly sent a cold chill up my spine. Never saw one like her in all my life. She had a build that would make a . . . . Well, I'll keep that thought to myself. One that many a young filly would envy and many a young man would kill to get a taste of."

"Better not let the misses hear that or there will be hell to pay," warned Langley.

Ignoring Langley's remark, Spred said, "That's about all I can tell you, except for one thing which I think you ought to know."

"What's that?"

"This is my own personal opinion, you understand," the storekeeper began. "I believe you are going to be dealing with one evil lady. I doubt if she knows what a conscience is. What I'm saying is this; when she and her companion came into the store, they bought enough grub to last a large party quite a while. Either they're going to eat a hell of a lot or feed a small army. Then, get this, she asked me to give her Bucklett's letter; you know the one to his wife. Can you believe that? I don't know how she knew about it, but believe me, that's the truth. Now, I know someday the government is going to permit a mail contract here in Tascosa, and I'd like to have it. I'm not going to jeopardize any chance of getting it. So I told her it had already been picked up and on the way to Fort Bent."

Spred's face got red with the memory. "Friend, that's when all hell broke loose, you'd of thought she turned into a witch who just had her broom stolen. She got hell-fire mad. Face got all white and shriveled up like a prune. She started cussing and raising hell like you wouldn't believe. For a minute there I thought she was going to come over the counter and cut my heart out. There's a river of bile flowing strong in that woman, believe you me."

With a quick glance toward Dain, Will said, "I don't recollect ever meeting anyone fitting their descriptions?" Dain shook his head.

"Do you remember any of their names?" Dain ask Spred.

"They didn't give any and I didn't ask. Her being madder than a tiger with his tail caught in a buzz saw, I wanted them out of my store, pronto."

The four men sat in silence, sipping their coffee.

Marshal Langley broke the stillness; clearing his throat, he looked at Will. "Bucklett, I wished I could help, but the way I see it, my hands are tied. There's not been any crime been committed that I can see. I'm not even sure it was Walker and Getchens who put that bullet in you. We've got no proof. Bedsides, I'm just a town marshal. I'm afraid you men are on your own.

"I rode out to their camp down on the river last night to question them, but they done pulled stakes. Personally, I believe they were the bushwhackers. But I've got to have more than just my personal assumptions before I can put out a notice on them."

"None of it makes any sense," Dain said, shaking his head.

Without a word, Will pushed back his chair and got up to leave. The other men followed.

"Where are you going?" Langley inquired.

"We're wasting time here," Will began. "Gentlemen, we're much obliged for the information you've given us. For all we know Pa could be dead already. If not, he definitely needs help. Personally, I think he's been kidnapped for some cockeyed reason. So, if you'll point us in the direction of Walker and his partner's camp, we'll be on our way."

"I'll do better than that; I'll ride along and show you." Langley said

"Appreciate that," Will said.

"What about your Indian friend?" Langley asked as they mounted.

"We'll cross his trail somewhere up the line," Dain assured him.

Will instantly approved of the animals Dain had acquired. The gelding he rode had three stocking feet, a blaze face, with a wide chest indicating strength, speed and endurance. But best of all Will felt like he was sitting in a rocking chair. Dain was astride a roan mustang, mountain-bred and trail-wise.

It was an unlikely campsite which Langley led them to. It was immediately obvious the two suspected gunmen selected the spot for neither comfort nor convenience. There was little cover and a good distance away from available water. It had been hastily deserted. Horse droppings and scattered debris indicated the two had settled down for a long wait on a small knoll, sparsely covered with mesquite. They found evidence the men took turns observing the comings and goings of Tascosa. The view was such that anyone entering or leaving the town could be seen from the selected vantage point.

"You might not have proof, Marshal," Will said as he swung astride the gelding. "But I'll tell you this. I've got all the proof I need to know that Walker and Getchens laid low, and waited for Dain and me to ride into your town. My guess is that once they made sure they had the right party, they set up to ambush us."

Langley settled in his saddle. "You may be right, Bucklett, but there's no way I could have known what they were up to, if it was Walker and his friend. We just don't know for sure," Langley scowled before continued. "Besides, you and Dain ride in and right away the shooting starts. I don't mean to be unkind, and I hope you find your father, but I'd just as soon you-all keep on riding."

"Just what I intend to do just as soon as I find what I want," Will said firmly.

"And what might that be?"

"I'm not sure at this point. Maybe another camp or wherever the trail leads me. I'll know when we see it."

Langley shook his head in frustration. "You'll find no other camp. I'd have knowledge of anyone within twenty miles of Tascosa. As for another trail, I doubt that seriously. Blowing winds on these high plains country will wipe out any tracks faster than a person can make them."

"We'll see," Will voiced confidently. "Thanks for all your help, Langley. Maybe our paths will cross again."

"Good luck to you both" Langley said in farewell. "But heed my warning. Don't try taking the law into you own hands; not in my jurisdiction, anyhow."

Dain and Will split up and started searching the area in a circle. Will worked the west in an arc, back and forth, north to south, then south to north. On each swing he went a little further out from the camp. Dain worked the east side in like manner. Each time they met in the center of the semi-circle, they would increase the radius, working further out. It was a slow and painstaking method, but necessary to cover the entire probable zone where one might situate a camp. Water was a deciding factor; an animal, especially horses, requires a lot of water. Since the Canadian River flowed west to east at this point, on the north side of Tascosa, it was reasonable to assume any encampment would lie somewhere within this region.

The probability of cutting the trail of the woman and her companions, or that of the two men their father was seen riding out of town with, was extremely slim, to say the least. There had been a blinding sandstorm through the country recently, and according to the townspeople, it had been over a month since Salas Bucklett was last seen riding off into the unknown. Patience was nothing new to the two mountain men. Moreover they had nowhere else to start. There was no discussion of Booger Red. He would do what he set out to do. They would cut his tracks somewhere up the line and catch up with him in due time.

As the day wore on, their eyes became reddened by the raw wind and occasional dust devils. Eyes were overly strained for a glimpse for the slightest clue. But the clue the brothers wanted most of all to see was some indication that Salas Bucklett was alive.

Will cut Booger Red's tracks early in the search. A short time later, he discovered a mound of rocks arranged to depict a message. To any other observer the stones would appear in their natural order. Only to the Buckletts and Booger Red did this illustration serve as an intelligent communication. "Red had picked up the trail of the two suspected shooters and would be on their trail. No help was required, and he would contact the brothers later. The two he followed were traveling fast and hard."

Will relayed the information to Dain when the met to share cold biscuits and a swig of water.

The western sky was beginning to lose its golden glow when at last Will heard two faint rifle shots. He topped a long ridge and saw Dain about a mile off to the north, waving his rifle. When Will joined his brother, they estimated they were some ten miles north of Tascosa. Together, they rode down a dry wash where Dain found recently made horseshoe tracks.

"Can't be sure, Will," Dain said hopefully. "But I'm pretty sure I've found the tracks of pa's mare going down this dry wash. See right here," he pointed. "It's an old one and filled some with sand. But I'm fairly positive that mare's been down this wash."

In a sharp, right hand bend of the wash beneath sandstone outcroppings, Will saw the welcome impression of several hoof prints. The tracks were out of the direct path of the wind stream which blew down the draw. A rider had apparently reined his mount over just enough to leave the tale-tale scars of a horseshoe imprint on the hardened sandstone jutting out from the side of the cliff wall.

"Hard to say, could be though. Have you been any further downstream?"

"No. I figured four eyes would be better than two. Don't want to miss anything."

Tying their horses to roots growing from of the bank, they slowly walked the bottom of the dry stream-bed cautiously in the direction the tracks were leading. They had been going only a short distance when perseverance paid off. Again the rider reined his mount to travel over a sandstone ledge protected from the windy draw. There, sufficient as Salas Bucklett's signature, lay a perfect track of a slightly pigeon-toed, right hoof prints of their father's mare so familiar to the brothers. Will and Dain, as young boys, had followed that track too many times over the rocky ridges of the Ozark Mountains to be mistaken.

As mountain-bred men, tracking men and animals was an instinct that had been honed in the pair since early childhood by Salas and Booger Red, two of the best. Countless times, one or both boys had been taken deep in the forest. Once there, they were left behind to live off the land and to find their way home, following signs left by the elders, the stars, and the lay of the land. Oftentimes it became an overnight trek. The boys survived off wild fruit, berries, vegetable roots, and small game caught by hand or snares. It was a school of hard knocks, being no older than they were, but an education they had learned to love and respect. However, instruction of the outdoors did not replace their education of reading, writing, and arithmetic. Amy Bucklett took care to see her boys could properly decipher the three R's.

Hopes lifted with the sight of the turned-in hoof prints. The red ball in the west was kissing the horizon when they came upon an abandoned campsite. The encroaching darkness forced their decision make camp upstream to await the morning to inspect the site. Both were impatient to discover the narrative the deserted campsite could disclose.

Will watched the small tongue of flame lick the sides of the battered coffee pot. For some reason the fire reminded him of the war. Probably because of all the senseless burning of homes and farms he had witnessed during those endless months before Appomattox. It seemed no matter which way he had turned, a blaze of consuming fire could be seen eating away some home, town, or countryside. Especially at night, the reddish glow of destruction could be viewed in all directions on the saw-tooth horizon.

His thoughts were disturbed as Dain, muttering incoherently, rose from frost-covered blankets. He wrapped his thread-bare blanket around his broad, square shoulders, and stepped in the edge of the ring of firelight, his back to Will.

"You know, Will, women have more of an advantage than we men do on cold, frosty night like this," Dain said with a chuckle in his voice.

"How's that, Dain?"

Dain was grinning as he fastened his trousers and returned to the campfire. "Well, one night during the war, it was so darn cold. This one night I was on a walking patrol, and my bladder was about to bust. So, I stopped, unbuttoned and bugger around trying to find it. You know if you're cold enough, it tries to crawl back up inside. Hell, I pulled out a hair and almost wet all over myself."

Will's burst of laughter triggered Dain's.

When their mirth had subsided, both began to reminisce about some of the happier, carefree days of their childhood.

*   *   *

The sun had not as yet showed itself as the brothers approached the abandoned campsite.

"Look here," Dain said as kneeled beside some blurred tracks. He pointed, "Here's where their horses were picketed. And there, that impression, it belongs to pa's mare. He's her shod recently, but no mistake about it. I'd know that print anywhere; I've seen it too many times."

Will had walked up an adjoining creek bed, intermittently laced with small pools of crystal clear water. "They're headed northwest; there are plenty of tracks leading that way. The way I read 'em, they don't seem to be in much of a hurry. I make it seven horses. The two sets of tracks cutting deep in the soil, I'd say, were the pack animals, and they were loaded down pretty heavy. More than likely the large amount of supplies Spred spoke of. That being the case, they're packing enough grub to last them a considerable spell."

As Dain continued to study the dead campfire, Will began searching slowly and cautiously around the outskirts of the camp. The need for all the information they could get on the group was increasing with each step. The remains a person leaves behind is often like his or her signature. Not an item discarded, an impression on the ground, nor any part of nature out of place could be overlooked.

"Dain you'd better come over here and take a look at this," Will said. He was standing close to a small cottonwood sapling, approximately six inches in diameter.

Near the base of the tree, bark had been chipped away. Lower down several blood splotches could be seen. The blood was obviously days old, dried and faded with time. The ground was markedly disturbed. There were impressions where boot heels dug deep into the ground. It was obvious a person, possibly wounded, had been tied to the tree, and had continually tried to push himself upright.

"What do you think happened here?" Dain ask, deep concern showed on his face.

Not wanting to unduly alarm Dain, Will said, "We won't know 'til we catch up to them . . . and then we may never know. You find anything over by the fire?"

"Just a lot of junk lying around, they didn't keep a very clean camp, that's for sure. Its plain they didn't figure on being followed, which could work in our favor. Just a lot of cigar butts, coffee rounds, tea leaves —"

"Tea leaves?"

"Yeah, someone is partial to tea. I'd say the woman or her companion. Two of the men wore boots with rundown heels. A third one had holes in his soles."

"The way I see it, they tied pa to this tree and someone was playing a dangerous game of dodging the bullet with him. I figure the blood—well, he was trying to get loose, and he rubbed his wrist so raw he started bleeding.

"Damn," Dain cried hotly, "They'll think 'playing game' when we catch up with them. I'm ready to ride, Will. They're playing for keeps and we're wasting time."

THREE

In a small cottonwood grove, two men huddled close to a blazing campfire which reflected dancing, shadowy figures on a rocky canyon wall. The men were dead tired, dirty, hungry and on edge. They had to leave Tascosa in such a hurry they had no time to stock up on supplies.

"I told you we should've got some grub to pack along," Bo Walker said disgustedly. "This is the last of the coffee, and there's nary a scrap of grub in our pokes."

"Aw, shut up," George Getchens replied hotly. "You do more bellyaching than a sack full of hogs at a pig killing contest."

"This is a fool's ride if I was ever on one. That uppity dude ain't gonna give us the rest of our money," Bo quipped. "And you're a knowing it the same as I do. We should be headed back to the Nations instead of trying to catch up with them. Most likely, they won't even be in Ludlow when we get there."

George watched his tobacco juice sizzle in the fire as he scratched his week old bread. "Look, all we got to do is ride into Ludlow, and tell them the Bucklett boys are buzzard bait. They'll believe us. We collect our fifty dollars and leave, making them think we've skedaddled back to the Nations. Then we hide out somewhere and when they leave Ludlow, we follow 'em. Don't worry, Bo, I've got it all figured out. They're onto something, and we're cutting ourselves in on the pot. If those two Bucketts show up, then maybe they'll just shoot it out and leave the way clear for us. Huh? What say? You with me? It could be our lucky break."

"Yeah, maybe. But it'll be a mighty long shot the way you're looking at it. I just don't like it," grumbled Bo. "Those folks don't appear to be nobody's fool."

"Don't worry about it. Just leave all the thinking to me."

George didn't want to push Bo. Bo had a short fuse. He had seen Bo's lightning fast draw, and he wanted no part of it. Not right now anyway. He'd wait until he had no more use for him. Right now he needed Bo to help carry out his plan.

"Let's turn in," George said soberly. "We still have a long haul ahead of us."

*   *   *

Booger Red had inched up to within twenty or so feet of the two ruffians' campfire, staying out of the ring of the glow. He had been lying there for the better part of an hour listening to the conversation between the two men.

So, Red reflected, Ludlow was where they were to meet the person or persons who had hired them to bushwhack Will and Dain. Who had hired them? Booger Red figured the reason they were hired to ambush the Bucketts was to prevent them from following Salas. He felt a need to inform the brothers, but first he must find out more information.

Red eased back about fifty yards and found where some animals had been bedding down in soft sand beneath a rocky overhang. He could still see the campfire and with a good view of the two men as they settled down for the night. He would wait here. Booger Red was good at waiting; it had become a part of his life.

The short, stocky one had already rolled up in his blanket; meanwhile the tall one threw more wood on the fire, sending a chimney of sparks high in the sky. Red shook his head at the foolishness and potential hazard of the white man's actions.

Later when Booger Red opened his eyes, dew had already begun to collect on the buffalo grass and the juniper trees. His estimated the time by the stars that it was well past midnight.

Like a cat stalking his prey, he moved from his cramped position and started toward the glowing coals of the dying campfire. With infinite care, he inched around the two sleeping men. He didn't know if they were light or heavy sleepers, but he was wise to the ways of those being hunted and the hunter. They would be wide awake at the snap of a twig, the stomp of a horse's hoof or the change of the wind.

With a feather-like touch, he snaked their rifles and six guns, and hid them behind a tree. They would probably have knives on their belts and maybe another weapon hidden on their body somewhere. But whatever other weapons they had would have to wait. He took up coils of rope of various lengths he had cut while waiting for them to off to sleep. He loosely looped an end of one rope around Bo's left leg near the boot; the other end he looped around George's right leg in like manner. For George's left leg, he made the same type of snare loop with another length of rope, looping it over a sucker limb of a nearby tree. With the remaining rope he looped it around Bo's right boot, and ran the rope through a fork in a cottonwood tree some ten feet away. He held both ends of the ropes he had thrown over the tree limbs in his hands. He observed, satisfied with his handiwork, he smiled. Both men were tied together at their boots, and he had the other ends of the rope arrangement in his hands. The men hadn't made a whimper during his movements.

Booger Red bunched his muscles, gave the two ropes a sudden, powerful jerk and pulled. Quickly, he tied his ends of the ropes to the stump of an old tree. Both men had been literally yanked into the air out of their sleep, and were now suspended in mid-air. They were spread eagle, upside-down splitting at the crotch like deer ready to be gutted. Savagely floundering in the entanglement of their blankets, they had no idea where they were or what was happened to them. Red quickly scooped up the knives, throwing them in the bush.

With their thrashing and clumsy struggling to get away from this bewildering predicament, the ropes became tighter. Booger Red had use snare knots and now the pain of their crotches became more intense. Hysterically, the two men began screaming and cursing at the top of their voices; ignoring the howling uproar, Booger Red began building up the fire.

"What the hell is going on here?" Screamed Bo Walker in a high-pitched voice which could have been heard a mile away. "I'm being split apart!"

"How the hell do I know, you idiot!" George yelled into the darkness. "Help get me out of this contraption before it kills me!"

Bo's answer to this plea for help was to scream curses blasting George's canine ancestry.

In an utter state of confusion, both men thrashed about, frantically clawing for something—anything to grab and hold on to, but there was nothing to be found, just plenty of empty air. To be awakened from a deep sleep in such a harsh manner was more than their simple minds could comprehend. The world was upside down, and all sense of sanity and direction had disappeared. George reckoned he was having a nightmare, and Bo was of a mind he had been swept up by a Texas twister had seen so frequently back in the Nations.

Booger Red watched the small flames leap to engulf the handful of small twigs that he threw on the dying fire, adding larger sticks as the flames took hold.

By the light of the glowing firelight, realization came to the men hanging by their heels. Slowly, recognition seeped through pain and confusion.

"It's that damned stinking Injun we saw in Tascosa," screamed Bo, twisting around to get a good look at Booger Red. Hysterically, he continued, "I'll kill him! I'll kill him! I'll skin that rotten buzzard and feed him to the hogs." Oh, he was mad. Mad enough to chew horseshoe nails.

George was too scared to say a word as he watched Booger Red get up slowly from his squatting position, pulling out his Arkansas pig-sticker. He grabbed George by the hair of the head, letting him have a good look at the razor-sharp double-edge twelve-inch blade. Red let go a high-pitched Indian screech that would curl the hair on a cougar's back.

"You talk. Fast. Plenty much."

"You're killing me, you damn heathen! Bo, do something, for God's sake! He's gonna scalp me!" George shrieked. The blood rushing to his head turned his face beet purple.

"You no talk, me open gut like deer." Red made a slashing motion with his knife. "Guts pour on ground; coyotes have good dinner on guts."

"I don't know—anything to tell,—damn you," George managed to say between gasps.

Booger Red chopped across George's nose with the hilt of his knife. His blood squirting on the ground brought a string of curses from George that would make a shanghaied sailor blush. Booger Red answered with an iron-like fist to the mouth. Grabbing George by the hair once again, Red grinned savagely and said, "If mouth no talk, keep shut. You lose more teeth."

Booger Red turned and stuck the point of the pig-sticker to Bo's neck, which drew blood instantly. "You like live, you tell why you shoot friend in Tascosa."

"Go to hell," Bo said stubbornly. Booger Red flipped his wrist in a quick downward motion. The razor-like tip caught Bo's chin, leaving a good half-inch gash. Blood flowed freely into Bo's upturned nose and mouth.

Flinging his head from side to side, spraying blood, Bo's fury turned into a fear that he had never known the fear of death. The events of Bo's life flashed through his mind in an instant. He saw his mother washing clothes over an old blacken kettle, his pa giving him his first whipping, the many battles of the Civil War. No one event of his life escaped the flashback of a dying man.

Unable to control the hysteria in his voice, Bo asked, "What do you want to know anyway?"

"Why you shoot Buckletts, like snake in grass."

"Got paid to make sure you all didn't leave Tascosa. We made a deal."

"Who pay?"

"I don't know just some people we met up with, a woman and a couple of hombres. We ain't ever seen 'em before. We were to wait in Tascosa and make sure you all didn't get any further. They didn't tell us anything else. Just to stop two white men and an Indian."

"You lie. What names? Where they go? You tell. You no tell; me split like pig."

"I don't know, damn it!"

Red let the knife point prick the neck, drawing fresh blood.

"Okay, okay, just get that knife away," Bo relented. "They were to give us a hundred dollars for the job. We were supposed to meet up with them in the Colorado Territory at a place called Ludlow, when the job was done."

"What names?" Booger Red asked.

"The woman they called Evie; and the tall gent went by the handle of Colonel John something or other, and there was a pea-eyed dude they called Tobe, or something like that, and a couple of other fellas. Gun hands, I figured. But it was the woman who hired us."

"Other two men, what names?"

"Don't know what their names was; we only seen them once. There was this big fella, his hand tied to the saddle horn and his feet tied to the stirrups. The two gunnies was guarding him all the time, real close like."

"Why man tied to saddle?"

"Don't know, damn it. Cut us down from here. I told you all I know. This ain't none of our business."

"You no tell all," Booger Red threatened. "You die."

"Damn you, Bo, he ain't funnin'! Tell him what it's all about before I bleed to death," cried George.

"All right, all right, damn it," Bo said faintly. "Seems that the big man they guarded knows where there's something they all want. I don't know what, but they want it powerful bad. I figure it might be he struck gold. Since he wouldn't tell them about his claim, they were taking him back to the high country with them. He is one stubborn old coot. He ain't talking or nothing, so they won't feed him, just enough water to keep him alive. If he doesn't die first, that old witch of a female might just cut his heart out and eat it. She's a mean one, she is. A she-devil if I ever saw one." Booger Red had disappeared silently into the darkness.

Terror gripped the two men at the thought of dying hanging upside down. Frantically, they began struggling against the ropes. Red returned after a few minutes leading the horses, and cut the two men down. Booger Red tied them to separate trees facing away from each other. Afterwards, he enjoyed a leisurely breakfast, oblivious to the insults and cursing from the ill-tempered gunmen.

The day wore slowly for Bo Walker and George Getchens. In the warmth of mid-afternoon, Bo awoke from a drowsy nap. From half-opened eyes he noticed Booger Red appeared to be asleep. Thinking he was hearing a soft snore, Bo took advantage of the opportunity to begin working on his bonds. As he worked at the ropes around his wrists, a sudden whoosh and immediate thump caused Bo to jerk his head around. Booger Red's Arkansas pig-sticker set, vibrating only inches above his scalp. Wide-eyed, Bo looked at Booger Red. Booger Red slowly lowered his head and instantly began to snore again. Bo gave up the idea of trying to escape. Maybe it would be better to work on his tied hands later, but not at this time. He had no doubt the half-breed would like the chance to use his knife again.

*   *   *

"See you caught yourself a couple of bushwhackin' varmints," Dain teased, swing down from the saddle.

"Weasels," Red corrected.

"They have anything to say?" Will asked.

"Some," Booger Red answered. He related to the two brothers what he had overheard and the information he had extracted from the two outlaws.

"Think they're telling the truth?" Will asked as he glanced at the two owl-hoots a good distance away.

"Have no backbone. This one no truth in him," he pointed to Getchens. "Me think have forked tongue. But other one, maybe one time." Red ran his thumb along the cutting edge of his eighteen-inch blade, shaking his head in doubt.

"Let's see," Dain stated. He untied his rope from his saddle, and commenced to walking toward the two men.

George, though still tied, began pushing himself upright against the tree. Fear etched his face as his eyes widened. "What you gonna do?"

"Nothing much, just gonna hang you boys," Dain spoke calmly.

"You can't do that. You're not the law," Bo said with a quiver in his voice.

"We're all the law that's needed around here," Said Will, firmly. "Besides, who's got a better right to hang you than us? You tried to kill us, you had your chance, should have done it to. I'm still carrying the hole one of you put in me. Now you've just got to suffer the consequences."

"We got nothing against ya'll," George whined. "We were just doing our job. We don't know you fellas from Adam."

"Hell of a way to make a living, going around shooting folks," Dain quipped.

"Honest to God, man, we told the breed everything we know. You'll find that bunch in Ludlow. We don't want any more to do with them folks. We done decided to head back to the Nations when your friend came up on us. Didn't we, George?" Walker lied.

George gulped, nodding his head vigorously, his eyes following the swinging noose Dain had tossed over an overhead limb.

"Why don't you tell us again? And, mister, it had better be the truth. I figure you're lying anywhere along the line, I'll yank this rope myself," Will said. The cold look he leveled at the two men left no room to doubt his sincerity.

Jumping at the chance to escape the hanging rope, Bo said, "Me and George was down on our luck, just sitting on our fanny down on the Red River Crossing, hoping to join up with a herd going through the Nations. This Colonel John and his lady rides up and offered us fifty dollars each for a month to ride along with them. That's a hell of a lot better wages than eating doggie's dust. So, we rode along. Finally, they promised us another hundred dollars to stop two men riding with an Indian coming through Tascosa. Course, after they left, we made up our minds to just sort of scare you some. But you must have jumped in the way. As God is my witness, I never meant to hurt you. That's the truth, if I ever told it, so help me. We never intended to kill or hurt nobody!"

"I'll just bet," Dain said doubtfully.

"Honest to God. That's the straight of it," Bo said pleadingly. "Anyway, in Tascosa, they met up with a kid; I think he must be that woman's brother. Tobe was his name. He stayed in our camp while the Colonel and Evie went into town. A couple of hours later they came back started packing their gear, like they're getting ready to move out. A little while later three other men rode in. The lady goes out to meet 'em. She tears in to the big fellas what has his hands tied, their hostage, giving him holy hell. She's' screaming at the top of her lungs. I've never seen anybody so mad. Then she comes back into camp, madder than a hellcat out for blood. Everybody shies away from her, getting real cautious like.

"Colonel John gave us a stake, and promised to meet in Ludlow who would give us the rest of our money after we finished the job."

Upon further questioning, Will and Dain came to the conclusion the two gunmen, although lying somewhat, knew little else of any great value.

They mounted up and rode west, taking a more northerly route. With luck they intended to make a stagecoach way station Booger Red remembered. There, they hoped to throw the two hardcases on the stage headed back toward Tascosa, and have the driver turn them over to Marshal Langley.

The sun had reached its zenith the following day when Booger Red informed they should make the way station long before dark.

They had about two more hours of sunlight as they were descending the long, slopping banks into the Purgatory River Basin. They'd been traveling the river southwest only a short time when they heard a splattering of gunfire.

"The way station!" yelled Booger Red.

"Can't be that far," Will said. "I'd estimate about a mile or so."

No more shots were heard for a few minutes, then suddenly all hell broke loose. A series of sporadic rifle fire echoed up the river basin.

"What do you make of it, Red? Sounds like someone in trouble?" Dain asked.

"Indians. Cheyenne. It their land." Booger Red explained.

"Let's tie these two to those cottonwoods down there, so we won't have to watch our backs. Sounds like those folks at the station can use a helping hand," Will said.

The three men had their horses belly flat to the ground as they rounded a bend in the river. Taking cover in a thicket of heavy brush, they scanned the terrain around the station. Two-hundred yards to their front stood the charred remains of what once been a freight wagon. Off to their left, set against an overhanging cliff was the adobe station with an attached horse corrals.

Using the remnants of the wagon for cover, six Cheyenne warriors whooped and hollowed as they tore into what had been the contents of the freight wagon.

What was once been a white man was tied spread-eagle to one of the remaining wheels of the wagon. His stomach was sliced open from his breastbone to below his navel. His entrails hung in a bloody, grotesque heap between his widespread bare feet, which were standing in the remains of a fire. The sickening smell of burning fresh was nauseating.

A young brave jumped from behind the wagon, shouted toward the adobe, turned and bared his buttock, and accompanied the motion with obscene gestures. Dust puffed near his feet as a shot rang out from the adobe. He sprang back for cover. Immediately another warrior drew another rifle shot from the opposite side of the wagon.

"They play with man in house," Booger Red surmised. "He no more bullets, they rush in, kill man in house."

"Look there, near the door," Will pointed. The body of a man lay face down near the entrance to the adobe. "Poor devil didn't quite make it. Whoever is in the house is putting up one hell of a fight."

Will was already sighting along the barrel of his rifle. In the space of a few seconds, the three men began laying down a deadly sheet of raining lead. Three of the unlucky warriors died in their tracks. The other three broke for cover of the river. An eagle feather suddenly flew into the air as the head to which it was attached exploded into countless pieces. The feather fluttered lazily to the ground as Booger Red's next bullet drilled into the kneecap of one of the last two braves. The last warriors leaped from the embankment onto a waiting pony.

"Look, one's getting away!" shouted Dain, as the sound of a single horse slapping the shallow stream of the Purgatory River.

"Him mine," Red assured him, digging his heels into his horse's flanks.

"Hello, the house," Dain cried out as he approached the adobe.

Dain watched as the door crept open slowly. A young girl, her eyes wide with skepticism, was holding a smoking rifle. She appeared somewhat baffled, as if she couldn't believe the fighting was over. Her deep blue eyes darted from Dain to Will and back again. Pushing back strands of long, black hair from an olive-tan, dirt-smudge face, she lowered her eyes to the body lying near the entrance. She paled. Dain thought she was going to faint, for she swayed momentarily. His heart went out to her as well as his hands.

"Are you all right?" His voice showed deep concern.

She turned to him, frowning, as if surprised at his presence. "Yes, thanks to you all. Where did you come from, and who are you?" She managed to say in a weak voice.

"I'm Dain Bucklett and that's my brother, Will Bucklett," Dain said, gesturing toward Will.

She dropped to her knees beside the body of the elderly man on the ground. Dain felt awkward, not knowing what to say or do. Finally, he walked to his horse and returned with a canteen of water.

Meantime, Will had cut the man loose from the wagon wheel and covered his body with what left of a tarp. He joined Dain who was some feet away from the girl.

"She's just a slip of a girl," Will asserted.

"Yep, she's just a girl," Dain agreed. "But she's just been through pure hell."

Dain walked over and put his hand gently on the girl's shoulder. "Come on, there's nothing you can do for him now. We'll take care of him. Don't worry," He said softly and compassionately.

She allowed herself to be led away, her head lowered. Dain wanted to ask who the dead men were, but it was too soon for such matters. She would tell them when the time was right.

"What's your name, Miss?" Will asked. He had covered the second body and approached the girl and Dain as she was taking the canteen from her lips.

"Trin. Trin Houghton," she answered. Her voice broke slightly, but still with a ring of strength. "He was my uncle." She indicated to the body near the cabin.

"You feel up to telling us what happened?" Will quizzed.

"They hit us just before noon. Jeb had just made it to the crossing yonder," Trin pointed to where the stage road crossed the Purgatory about half-mile upstream. "Suddenly, they came up over the embankment. They must have been hiding down in the brush. Poor Jeb, he never had a chance. He was bringing winter feed for the stock. Uncle Everett started to run out and help him, but . . . The Indians were all over Jeb before Uncle Everett got ten feet out of the cabin. I yelled at him to come back. He saw he was too late to help Jeb and he started running back. That's when he got—he never . . . ." Trin's voice broke, her small body racked with heart-wrenching sobs.

Booger Red rode into the yard in a swirl of dust. "They go!" he declared.

Trin's face lost its color when she saw Booger Red. She started to raise her rifle.

"No! He's a friend." Dain pulled the rifle down.

"That's okay, Red," Will assured him, thinking Red was speaking of the lone Indian who had escaped. "We'll be pulling out before he can be coming back with his friends."

"No! Cheyenne now in spirit world," he pulled his hand flat across his throat. "Two white man, they go. Escape."

"Damn it," Will exclaimed. "Well, they're most likely halfway back to the Indian Territory by now."

"No," said Booger Red. "They go toward sun." He pointed west.

Dain looked at Will. "Will, if they beat us to Ludlow, they'll warn that gang, whoever they are. If that happens and they take off to the mountains, we may never find pa."

"Never have to worry, Dain. There are not enough places in those mountains to hide, where another Bucklett can't find another Bucklett," Will tried to sound reassuring.

"Who did you say?" Trin asked.

"Bucklett," Will turned toward her. "That's our name, Bucklett. Salas Bucklett is our father. We're dang near positive he has been taken prisoner for reasons we're not sure of. We're fairly sure they're headed for those mountains yonder."

"No!" Trin exclaimed loudly. "Oh, please, no."

FOUR

"Do you know our father?" Will stared, stunned by her reaction.

"Oh, yes," Trin began. Her eyes filled with tears. "He and Uncle Everett were the best of friends. Actually, more like brothers than friends. Uncle Salas is like family. He was always bringing us things when he dropped by." She stopped suddenly, gasping, "Then you all must be . . . I'm sorry I just didn't make the connection when you told me your names before," Trin rubbed her eyes. "Yes, Will and Dain. He's told us so much about you men and Mrs. Bucklett."

"Yeah, that's us," Will said in complete surprise.

"And your Indian friend over there, he must be Booger Red. Where's your mother?"

"She passed away some weeks back." Will said. "After we buried her, we came west looking for our pa. We traced him as far as Tascosa,

Texas. We're pretty sure he came this way, although, not of his own free will. By all accounts, we believe, he was taken prisoner by a man we desperately want to meet up with."

"I think I know the man you're talking about. In fact, I saw him once. If it's the man I'm thinking about, his name is John Bullard. I think he use to be a colonel in the Union Army. He and another man came by our place only a few weeks ago looking for Uncle Salas. Uncle Everett told them he had no idea where Salas was. He got very angry. He didn't believe Uncle Everett and said as much. He made some wild threats, of sorts. And from what Uncle Salas said he can be a very violent and unscrupulous person," Trin said with a shudder.

As Booger Red and Dain joined them, Dain said, "We're ready."

Will nodded, looking at Trin, "We'll talk later," he motioned toward the graves Red and Dain had readied.

* * *

The rays of the rising sun were welcome warmth on the backs of the small party of four as they rode west toward the town of Ludlow. Wanting to put as much distance as possible from the stage station. They had ridden well into the night, finally stopping to make a fireless camp and a brief few minutes of rest. The likelihood of the lone Indian which had gotten away, bring back some of his friends was too great to stick around. And there was always the chance another party of Cheyenne could be in the area.

Predawn again found them traveling westward toward the front range of the Rockies. The two brothers shared with the others their first view of the Rocky Mountains being unveiled by the vivid morning sun. They watched with astonishment the achievement of God's beautiful ever-changing handiwork. The intense brightness of the twin snow-topped Spanish Peaks set against the fading darkness of the westward moving night increased to a hypnotic white. The lower foothills were sharply outlined against the extraordinary hue of blue of the distant peaks. Suddenly, as if God had snapped his fingers, the unveiling was complete. The mountains before them and the surround landscape were engulfed in glowing, brilliant sunlight. The high country air was crisp, sharp and incredibly clear, visibility unlimited.

As Will watch the fabulous panorama, he felt a sense of belonging. A kinship. A place to put down roots, to dream dreams and bring them to fruition. He understood what his father had told him long ago. "It's a country of unbelievable beauty, with majestic mountains reaching to the deep blue sky. Each mountain is like an exotic woman, calling, beckoning to ascend her heights,"

Trin rode up beside him, "It's beautiful, isn't it?"

"I've seen the Blue Ridge and the Alleghenies, but never anything which could be compared to those," Will pointed.

"See that halo of clouds off to the north there? That's Pike's Peak. Uncle Everett, he . . ." She choked back the memory of her slain uncle. She continued, haltingly, "He said the Peak is more than fourteen thousand feet high. Can you imagine? He and Uncle Salas took me with them to the Maestas Ranch a long time ago, and I got to see Pike's Peak up close. It's magnificent."

Will glanced admiringly at Trin as they rode in silence. This girl had strength, he thought. Having lost her only living relative and benefactor, she wasted little time on things she could not control. A true product of the west; she knew the art of survival. Her uncle had taught her well. There was no grumbling, no complaining. She knew what had to be done and got on with it.

"You don't mind, do you?" Trin asked shyly, breaking the rhythmic beat of the hooves against the grassy plains.

"What?"

"You don't mind me calling your father Uncle Salas, do you?"

"I'm pleased you think so highly of him; I'm sure he's proud to be so called," Will said with a smile.

"You think he's okay? I mean, you don't think they'd really hurt him, do you?" Trin frowned, her eyes showing her apprehension.

"I really don't know what to think. I doubt if anything will happen to him as long as they think he's got something they want," Will paused, forcing a smile. "Besides, he's a tough old bird. He'll be okay." Will wished he could feel the assurance he was attempting to give Trin.

The sun was high in the sky when they were joined by Dain, who had been riding rear guard, just in case. "Seen anything of Red?" Dain asked, looking forward along the trail.

"Saw him as he went over the rise yonder, a while back. Apparently he hasn't seen anything to be concerned about, or he would have let us know," Will informed him.

"I don't think we're being followed. If we are, they're a good ways back," Dain assured them. Smiling at Trin, he continued. "It must have been a hunting party just as you and Booger Red figured."

"If you feel up to it, Trin, we'd like to hear all you can tell us about Colonel Bullard," Will said, glancing from under his hat.

"There's really not much I can tell you. Just listening to Uncle Salas and Uncle Everett talk, they say Colonel Bullard is a very vindictive and ruthless individual. I might be wrong, but I believe all this may have something to do with a shipment of Union gold.

"Understanding Uncle Salas and Uncle Everett when they were in conversation was often a bit trying." Remembering, a slight smile touched Trin's lips. "They were either talking at the same time or cutting each other off, trying to get a word in edgewise. The more I tried to listen and understand, the more confused I became."

"What's that you were saying about a gold shipment?" Dain asked.

"Well, it was a long time ago, during the war," Trin began. "Uncle Salas came by our place one night, and he and Uncle Everett talked long into the wee hours. They were talking about a plan the Confederates had to raid a Union gold shipment and turn it over to the Confederate Army. That's when we lived in Dodge City. A couple of days later they left and were gone about a month. Then late one night I heard a wagon pull into our yard. I looked out the window, because Aunt Ellen had told me to stay in my room. They were pulling the wagon into the barn. When I went down to breakfast the next morning, Uncle Everett was setting there as if he had never left. I asked him about Uncle Salas; that's when he made me promise that if anyone ever asks, I hadn't seen him."

"The South sure could've used the money," Will said. "You ever see Pa again? After that, I mean."

"He came when he heard Aunt Ellen died. That was a few months later," Trin answered. "But about a week after Uncle Everett came back from his trip with Uncle Salas, we had some late night visitors, four cowboys who were on their way back to Texas. Aunt Ellen fed them and talked their ears off about Texas. Well, anyway, they went out to the barn with Uncle Everett and stayed a good while. It was late, I guess about midnight, and I heard the cowboys ride off. Later, I asked Aunt Ellen what it was all about, and all she said was, "They were friends of Uncle Salas, and they came to pick up something that Uncle Everett was holding for him." Sometime later I heard him talking to Aunt Ellen, and he was saying "it" would help shorten the war. Whatever that meant, I don't know."

"You never saw or have any idea what it was they took away?" Dain asked.

"No," she said, shaking he head. "I could only guess."

"Gold?" Dain said.

"That would be my guess," she said.

"Gold the South needed desperately to continue fighting the war," Will added. Looking at Dain, he continued, "Could be there's a little bit of that war still going on."

"Appears to be, if you're thinking what I think you're thinking," Dain answered.

Will grabbed his hat against a gust of threatening wind. "Trin, you said there was another man with Bullard. Is there anything you remember about him?"

"No, not really. It was near sundown when they came. The light was behind them, and I really didn't get a good look at their faces. Besides, Uncle Everett made me stay in the house. It was a scary few minutes, if you know what I mean."

They rode in silence for a few minutes.

"It's not important right now," Will began, "But I . . ." He suddenly realized he was talking to himself.

Will looked around and saw that Trin and Dain had dropped a considerable distance behind, and were conversing in low tones. He smiled as he remembered the way they had been cutting eyes at each other while breaking camp this morning. He had been surprised that Dain had ridden rear guard as long as he had.

They came upon Booger Red squatting near the crest of a sloping rise. The landscape was beginning to change. Sparse cedar scrubs and pinion dotted the surrounding countryside.

"Ludlow," Booger Red pointed to the ribbon of smoke hanging lazily on the pale blue horizon.

"About an hour's ride, I'd say," Will commented as Dain and Trin rode up. "We'll rest the horses here, for a while."

Trin began drawing lines in the sand. "There's a mercantile, it also serves as the ticket office and mail room for the stage line, which use to run from Trinidad to Walsenburg. But I don't know even if it does now or not. Then there's a blacksmith lean-to that connects the livery to the store. Across the road and south of the livery, there's a white little house where Pete and Fran live."

"Pete and Fran, they take care of the place?" Dain asked curiously.

"Yes," Trin answered. "They've only been here a short while. Ludlow was once thought to be a promising coal mining town, but the coal played out real quick, Uncle Everett said. Uncle Everett and Uncle Salas knew Pete from their trapping days. Fran is a Northern Cheyenne, daughter of Twisted Nose, a sub chief. None of the tribes around here would dare harm them. She is very beautiful and a very special friend."

"Let's swing off to the right and come in from the north. If Bullard and his friends are there, they'll more than likely have lookouts posted for anyone coming from the east or south, especially, if Walker and his pal have beat us here. Could be they wouldn't be suspicious of riders coming in from the north on the main road in." Will said, "At least, that's my way of thinking."

"How often does the stage make the run?"

Her gaze was soft toward Dain, "Use to be about once a week, but that was some time ago."

They came upon the north-south road some five miles north of town. There was no street to speak off, just the stage road running straight through to Trinidad. The blacksmith lean-to, livery barn and corral all seemed to be connected to the mercantile. The entire building faced the west from the east side of the road, the mercantile, the blacksmith shop, and the livery stable—just one long slapdash construction. Will took note that the mercantile also served as the saloon as well. Across from the livery barn and corral, some two-hundred yard further south, stood a small white clapboard house. Must be where Pete and his Indian wife lived, Will thought.

There was no sign of life as their horses kicked up powder dry dust from the little used stage road.

Billowing clouds began building rapidly over the foothills and mountain tops to the west as the four entered the north end of town as the swirling dust announced the possibility of a storm.

"Looks mighty quite," Dain commented. "That's not to my liking."

A relay team of six horses stood, tails switching in the pole corral. A shaggy, yellow dog came running out to sniff the heels of the newcomers. A sudden gust of wind came out of nowhere to pivot a squeaky windmill before dying after turning half a turn. There was no other sign of life or activity.

"That's not unusual," Trin said in response to Dain's comment. "Pete would be spending a good deal of time at home with Fran when no stage is due. They're probable at home, I'll run down and say hello." She heeled her horse into a gallop.

"You be careful now," Dain called after her.

"Don't worry. They're good friends of ours," she called over her shoulder.

Will and Booger Red smiled knowingly at each other.

Dain's face flushed crimson red as he noticed their grins. "Well, what the heck, she's a right pretty girl."

"Oh," Will said with raised eyebrows, "I hadn't noticed."

"Besides, she's got no more family now that her uncle's gone," Dain countered.

"You taking on the job looking out for her, are you, Dain?" Will teased.

"She could do worse, Brother," Dain noted proudly. "She could do worse."

"I must say, you have a point, but first thing first, Dain," Will reminded him as he stepped down from the saddle.

"Man who loses heart to woman is like a trapped animal," Booger Red said, taking the reins of the ponies. "I water horses."

As Will and Dain entered the store, the wind had suddenly increased coming in off the foothills. The canyon's wall often acted as a funnel to any breeze coming from the west.

A few bales of fur sat in one corner of the large room. The left side of the room served as the mercantile, with shelves stacked with can goods, barrels of flour, some sacks of salt, beans, and other odds and ends. A few slabs of salted bacon hung from a wooden beam running the length of room. A pot-belly stove sat next to a table, roughly hewn from local timber, as were some benches and cane bottom, straight back chairs. Some tacks and other leather good, a man was likely to need hung haphazardly around the room. A small cubical enclosed with hog wire at the rear apparently served as the post office. On the wall opposite the mercantile stood the bar, which consisted of two four-by-eight planks lying across two empty whiskey barrels. Half a dozen or so liquor bottles were line up on wooden crates behind the made-shift bar.

Will thought the place seemed like a place a trapper would come for supplies more than that of a stage relay station. He elbowed Dain, nodding to the freshly spilled whiskey on the bar, some still dripping onto a puddle on the floor. Dain nodded his head in understanding. Cautiously, he approached the double-swinging doors at the end of the bar leading to the blacksmith shop.

"Quiet," Dain observed.

"Too damn quiet," Will agreed, strolling to the cage at the rear of the room. "Yet someone left in one hell of a hurry, I'd say."

The wind was now beginning to rattle the building with enormous gusts. Choking dust filled the room. A windmill began to groan, slowly at first, and then the squealing picked up speed as the increase of wind pushed more forcefully against the sails. Somewhere an open door slammed shut, and then squeaked mournfully, swinging on rusty hinges.

Will peered into the hog-wired cage that served as a post office. There was little doubt in his mind that the man lying on the wooden floor behind the enclosure was dead. Not only was his face battered beyond recognition, but there was a hole in his chest the size of a man's fist. It was apparent he had been shot in the back. The bullet's exit had made one hell of a hole.

"We're . . ."

His next words were cut off by an ear-piercing scream, causing both men to voice simultaneously.

"Trin!" Dain Yelled. He hit the door running with Will right behind him. But skidded to a halt as he stepped off the porch into the dirt roadway before the mercantile.

Three men came toward them from the direction of the clapboard house across the road. It wasn't hard to figure out which of the three was Colonel Bullard. The officer's cavalry hat and riding pants stuffed into high top, black boots set him apart from the two hardcases on either side of him.

Trin walked in front of Bullard who had a hand full of her hair knotted at the back of her head. Her head was pulled back, chin up. Her high-pointed breasts strained against the worn fabric of her thin cotton shirt. The cotton shirt had been partially pulled from the homespun trousers she wore, exposing portions of her undergarments.

"Easy, Dain," Will cautioned as they came within earshot. In Bullard's right hand, he held a pistol to Trin's head.

"Good advice, Bucklett," Bullard's voice was soft and watery, like he had a mouth full of salvia, but couldn't spit.

"It would be rather foolish for either one of you to try anything out of the ordinary. I can assure you I will not hesitate for one moment to kill this beautiful, desirable, young lady if either of you should do so."

Bullard's viciously tightened his grip on Trin's head preventing any voluntary movement. Her eyes were wide, pleading as she glanced from one to the other of the brothers. There she saw fury and knew it was not directed at her, but to her attackers. Trin hoped they wouldn't try any heroics. She was furious for allow herself to be responsible for the present situation.

Looking at Dain, Bullard warned, "I don't like the look in your eyes, young man. You so much as blink and she's a dead woman."

Will's eyes were locked with those of the man on Bullard's right. Recognition furrowed Will's brow. The man had changed drastically since the war, but he wasn't surprised. Hard living ages a man mighty fast. Hard lines sat deep along the man's temples. His dark, sinister eyes had the look of a caged, wide animal, constantly preparing to strike at anyone or anything without any provocation whatsoever.

"Drop those rifles easy and unbuckle your gun belts," Bullard's word brought Will's thoughts back to the present.

As he retrieved the weapons, Elkhart brought his face to within inches of Will's. Will felt a hard poke of cold steel against his ribs. The man's breathe, foul with stale tobacco and rotting teeth, mixed with the stench of his unwashed body was nauseating.

"Remember me, do you?" Elkhart sneered maliciously.

"How could I forget a maggot-infested polecat?" Will answered.

"You two know each other?" Bullard quizzed.

"Yeah, I know the rebel scum," Elkhart declared. "I said we'd meet again, Bucklett. Now I'm going to empty your wagon, just like I promised," Elkhart smiled wickedly, thumbing back the hammer of his pistol.

"Not now," ordered Bullard. Ice was thick in his voice. "Later. We take care of business first. Then you can have him all to yourself. There's too much at stake here to blunder away."

Elkhart began to laugh, lowering the hammer on his revolver, "Yeah, all right. I can wait, and while I'm waiting, you think on it, Reb. You're going to die a slow death."

Bullard shoved Trin forward. She stumbled into Dain's arms. He wrapped them around her protectively.

"They killed Fran," Trin managed to say, her head against Dain's shoulder.

He started to tell her Pete's body was inside, but decided she had more than enough to cope with now.

"Where's our pa?" Will demanded, looking intently at Bullard. "And what do you want of him, or us? And by all that's Holy, he'd better be okay."

"All in good time, my friend," Bullard vowed. Not taking his eyes off Will, he commanded, "Sheet, get those other two nitwits from the barn."

Bullard's smile was frigid, "Your old man is a very stubborn individual. Normally, that is a quality I admire, but not at this point in time. So, with the cooperation from little brother here, Salas is going to make me a very rich man. Yes, sir, a very rich man indeed."

"Makes us rich!" Elkhart corrected him sternly.

"Well, yes, of course. I meant to say all of us on this expedition. Just a slip of the tongue, I assure you," he smiled wolfishly at Elkhart.

If Elkhart believed the colonel, it didn't show in his expression. "Just make damn sure you remember that."

Turning to Dain, Bullard said, "Your father is in good company and in good health, as you will soon see, young man. You're going to accompany us to where he now—shall we say, resides. And you will, if you know what's good for all of you, convince him to disclose the location of us—shall we say a certain missing chest of Union gold. If not . . ."

"Gold?" Dain interrupted. "Pa doesn't have any gold, and never has had any? Hell, we've never had a pot to piss in much less gold. You're crazier than a cockeyed coon on a stormy night."

Bullard's expression reminded Will of a deadly coiled rattlesnake. His eyes marked Dain for immediate elimination from the face of the earth.

"We'll play your game, Colonel," Will, interjected sharply, laying a hand on Dain arm. "You're holding all the cards, for now." Will thought hurriedly, knowing Dain's short temper, not wanting the situation to get out of control. Not only for their father's sake, but there was Trin and Booger Red to think of. There had been no sign of Booger Red. Was it possible the colonel's men had missed him as they had ridden into town? Not likely. Still, the fact that Booger Red hadn't been mentioned puzzled Will. However, if there was some slim chance they had missed him, it would be very unwise to expose his presence by asking about him. Will hoped Dain and Trin were thinking along those same thoughts. Otherwise, he could only assume his friend was just biding his time to assist them.

He felt slightly relieved as Bullard seemed to gain some sense of composure. He noticed also, that Dain seemed to relax somewhat as he, too, sensed the man's instant transformation. Cautiously, Will added, "I'd like to make this suggestion. I should be the person to accompany you instead of my brother. He and Pa never did see eye to eye. So, if you could give me a little more detail of what you're after, I believe I would be able to convince Pa to cooperate."

"Oh, no, I . . ." Dain began.

"You're damn right; I'm holding all the cards, and it's a pat hand. You both will do well to remember that, especially you, young man," Bullard stared hard at Dain. Turning back to Will, he said, "Dain will go with us as I have instructed. You and the girl will stay here. Of course, you will be under guard. I can't permit you to get in the way of my operation. I don't want to kill the lot of you, or any of you, for that matter. But, I will not let you disrupt my plans. I hope that's understood. I shall do what I have to do. I will not be stopped.

"However, maybe it would be best if you knew just what the stakes are. You might then understand why I'm so adamant in my endeavors. You see, during the war, your old man and a bunch of rebel riffraff took—stole is a better word—a chest of gold that had been entrusted to my care. That dishonorable deed caused me a great deal of embarrassment, not to mention the termination of my promising military career. Nevertheless, all can be forgiven if this certain chest were to be placed back in my hands forthwith."

"Salas Bucklett was a Major of the Confederate Army man serving a cause he believed in," Will said. "A military man such as yourself. And I'm positively sure that if he was responsible for taking this gold you speak of, or whatever it was, it was only in the line of duty. And he would have turned it over to the Confederate government. He was no thief, I can tell you that. Anyway, whatever it was, even if it was gold, it has most likely been turned over to the proper authorities."

"No, you naive fool," Bullard told him. "I have friends in high places. That particular chest has never surfaced. The ex-Major Salas Bucklett knows exactly where it is. I'm positive of that."

Will was not surprised to see Bo Walker and George Getchens approach from the direction of the barn. A tall slim cowboy, Will assumed to be Sheets, trailed behind the two gunmen.

All three were grinning like possums in a persimmon tree. Will knew very well those grins would be bad news.

Turning to the two hardcases, Bullard slowly and distinctly said, "I'll give you blundering idiots another chance. I'll spell it out in simple terms. You are to keep Bucklett and the girl here until you hear from me. That's all, just keep them here."

"Yes, sir, Colonel," George said enthusiastically. "You can count on us. Can't he, Bo?"

"Damn better, if you want to be cut in on this deal," Bullard growled. "Now tie them up so we can get started. Elkhart, gives them a hand, and make sure they'll stay secure."

He saw Will and Dain exchange glances. "Don't even think about it. With five guns on you, you wouldn't stand a snowballs chance in hell. And the girl would be the first to go."

The horses were led from inside the clapboard house. Bullard had thought of all the details to hide their presence and to make the small town seem normal.

There was a very good possibility that Dain would be in a position to assist their father if Bullard had spoken the truth. Will was thankful that Booger Red had restrained from showing himself. Otherwise, all hell might have broken loose, and they wouldn't have learned what the colonel was up to. For now it seemed best to go along with whatever the colonel had in mind. At least we had an ace in the hole, which was Booger Red. Or did we?

FIVE

Dain sat astride his horse, guarded on either side with Skeets on the right and Elkhart on his left. He watched helplessly as Will and Trin hands were securely tied and led into the mercantile. Casually, he looked around; slightly surprised Booger Red had been able to stay out of sight. The surrounding landscape lay flat as a flapjack for more than a mile in every direction. There was no evidence their companion ever existed.

The brothers had exchanged looks of encouragement and assurance before Will and Trin were led away. Dain frowned as he noticed Bullard and Getchens stood on the porch in a whispering conference. He had a bad feeling, trying in vain to overhear what they were discussing.

Whatever instructions Bullard left could not have been good, at least for the Bucketts. Bullard had a sinister smile on his face as he donned his ankle length duster.

Bullard glanced momentarily at Dain, "Do I have your word that you will not try to escape?"

"Now that's a stupid question," Dain sarcastically. "We came all this way to find our pa. You know where he is; I don't."

"Good, then we have an understanding. We'll forgo tying you to the saddle horn, but give me any trouble and I'll change my mind." Bullard's expression changed slightly as he noticed the building thunderhead over the mountains to the west. "Let's get going. There's a storm brewing. There'll be hell to pay if we get caught in it."

*   *   *

Will flexed his hands and wrists, trying to ease the pain of the tight binding, as well as testing the ropes. After the colonel and Dain left, Walker and Getchens retied him with his arms around a large support pole in the center of the room. On quick observation, Will saw it was the only support of a twelve-inch beam which ran the length of the room. The beam was use to hang smoked meat and such. On top of the beam, planks had been laid butting end to end. The other ends of those planks were supported by the outside walls. The idea of moving the pole to bring down the center was quickly discarded. There was no way he would be able to jar the pole, even if he was free to try.

Walker and Getchens were engaged in a low toned conversation near the door with their backs to him. When Getchens went outside, Walker followed him to the door. With Walker's back to him he tested the support for any movement. To his utter disappointment there was not the slightest budge, as solid as if it had roots.

Trin sat dejectedly on a bale of fur, her hands tied securely behind her back. Bo Walker walked over, checked her bindings, leaned on the dusty plank bar and tilted a bottle of whiskey to his lips. Trin shivered under his lewd stare.

"You think you're too damn good for me, don't you?" The amber liquid dribbled from the corner of his sneering lips into his matted beard. "When George gets back in here, we're going to show you a thing or two," he paused, laughing boisterously. "Somethin' you ain't never seen before, I'll bet."

"Let her alone, Walker," Will ordered. "Can't you see she's just a girl child?"

"Yeah, and what a girl. Besides, what's it to you?" His eyes widened. "Oh ho, hey, she's been warming your blankets, huh?" Walker strutted in front of Will. Smiling, he thumbed back the hammer of his battered old pistol and placed the muzzle against Will's nose. "What you gonna do about it, huh? I'll tell you what you're gonna do about it. Nothing. You ain't gonna do one damn thing."

Walker threw back his head and bellowed with laughter. Holstering the old Remington .44, he turned and approached Trin. She began visibly shaking as Walker clutch her chin between callused fingers. She tried to pull away, but Walker was expecting her reaction. He pushed her further back upon the pales of pelts. Her heaving, high-pointed breast pressing against the old cotton dress caused one of the buttons to pop off. Walker seemed to go into frenzy; he stared, bug-eyed, drooling, and eager with anticipation.

"Get away from her, you damn leech!" Will cried out. "Or I'll . . ."

"Or you'll what?" George Getchens said entering the room. He drove a hammer like fist into Will's kidneys, dropping him to his knees. The searing, blinding pain brought tears to his eyes. His eyes fluttered open to see Getchens brutal grin revealing stained teeth, but too late to escape the sharp-pointed boot that smashed wickedly into his ribs.

Will shook his head, fighting off the dizziness. His ears were ringing violently, mingling with the quarreling going on between Walker and Getchens. Gradually, he forced his eyes to focus.

"Oh, no," Getchens was saying. "You can have her when I'm done with her, and not before."

"Like hell, you say!" Walker hollered.

Trin lay between the two men. Tangled hair covered her face. Racking sobs shook her small, delicate frame."

'Yeah, like I say!" Getchens shouted, menace in his voice. He shoved his cocked pistol into Walker's ribs. "I've had just about a belly full of your pissin' and moanin', Walker. You say one more damn word, and I'm going to blow your guts to kingdom come."

Walker retreated. He wasn't ready to die, and he was staring death in the face. "Aw, okay, I was just funn' anyway. Don't get your bowels in an uproar. Just don't hurt her too much. I like 'em with a little spirit in 'em."

Through clenched teeth, Will exhaled against the sharp pain. "You'll never get away with this, you low life piece of scum. When . . ."

"When what?" Getchens cut him off. "You think your half-breed friend will be coming to help you? Why, you two-bit dumb sodbuster. We've done took care of your heathen brother, didn't we, Walker?"

"You damn come a-tootin'," Walker gloated gleefully. "Strung that red sucker up like a stuck hog. He damn sure got what was coming to him. He won't pull no more fool stunts."

Will roared furiously and strained against the ropes. He wanted desperately to reach the two men. He felt the skin on his wrists tear; his hands became sticky with his own blood. A battering blow to the side of the head left him dazed. He had to think. He must stay conscious; it was a trying effort just to think and concentrate.

Will reasoned that, apparently, Getchens and Walker had been hiding in the barn as they rode into town. It was inconceivable that Booger Red fell in a trap just as he and Dain had. But it happens to the best, he reflected to himself, no matter how careful one tries to be. Now, assuming there would be no help from Booger Red, it's all up to me, he thought. There's no one else. No outside help will be coming. His mind raced for a solution, a way out. Presently and firstly, he feared for Trin now more than anyone else. One thing was for sure, he watched Getchens carefully. The man had just about reached the end of his rope, and there's no telling when that rope would snap.

"While I take little missy down to the house," Getchens told Walker, "You hunt up some coal oil."

"Why?"

"Orders, that's why!" Getchens shouted angrily. "We're going to burn this two-bit burg to the ground before nightfall. That's what the colonel wants, and it'll be my pleasure." He paused; his cruel eyes darted between Will and Trin, grinning wickedly. "And after we've had some fun with this little filly, there's going to be an accident. Then we'll meet up with the colonel and collect our share."

"Where?" Walker wanted to know.

"Never mind where. Just get the coal oil and have it ready," he turned toward Trin with a leer. "When I'm finished with her, I'll give you a call. You make damn sure he is well tied before you come down," he nodded toward Will.

"Why don't we just shoot him right here and now?" Walker grinned. "I'd be real obliged."

"The colonel wants it to look like the Indians done it, stupid."

"Don't call me 'stupid,'" Walker said furiously.

Getchens walled his eyes. "Come on, missy. Let's go play." He grabbed Trin's shirt and yanked. The remaining buttons gave way. More creamy skin was exposed, causing both men to gasp.

Trin struggled to turn away. "Don't. Please don't do this," she pleaded.

Walker stepped forward and ripped her cotton underwear apart. "Sweet mother of . . . ." he cried out. "Look at them beauties. Hurry, George. I ain't had me a woman in a coon's age and never one like her."

Trin strained, trying desperately to pull away and cover herself, not realizing her actions only served to further excite both men.

Will was overcome with guilt and frustration at his inability to come to her aid in anyway whatsoever. Contemptuously, he cried out, "I swear to God, you are both dead men!"

Getchens laughed cruelly as he shoved Trin stumbling toward the door. She tripped and fell to her knees, somehow managing to modestly cover herself in a fashion. Getchens grasped her by the hair, jerked her upright and forced her through the door into the street. The groan escaping Trin's lips haunted Will.

Will's eyes swept around the room. He had a fleeting moment to attempt to reason with Walker; just as quickly, the thought was discarded.

Getchens had confidently left his twelve-gauge, double-barrel shotgun lying on the bar as he searched for coal oil. Will took note that he had holstered his six-gun while he was rummaging around in the mercantile goods. Will reasoned the coal oil was to create a blazing inferno death bed for Trin and himself.

He knew he had precious little time to lose if he was going to be of any help to Trin. As if to answer his thoughts, he heard Trin scream.

Walker stopped momentarily to listen, his back to Will. Will grasped the pole and gave it a sharp tug. No movement. He crouched. Hugging the pole with all his strength, if I can just lift it a mite, he thought. Assuring himself he wasn't being observed, he bunched his body and strained with all his power. He muscles, unaccustomed to such an awkward position, straining to the point of being ripped apart. But the pole moved. He was elated. It could be brought down. But he didn't have much time. Trin was in terrible danger. Bracing his six-foot-two, two-hundred twenty-two pounds frame of rock hard muscle, he rolled up and back with every fiber of his being. The aged timber groaned. Walker turned suddenly, staring intently at Will.

The escalating wind gust was the only disturbance to the heavy silence. A sudden blast of wind caused the old building to groan, breaking the stillness. Will held his breath, his heartbeat quickened. But Walker resumed his search; Will gave a sigh of relief and looked overhead. One of the rough hewn planks of the loft floor threatened to dislodge at the slightest movement. He was now sure he could cause the loft to collapse, but how to get Walker under the heavy beam was the question. He had to come up with something fast. A plan quickened, but could he keep from getting himself pinned under the beam along with Walker, he wondered. Each passing second stretched to an unbelievable moment in time.

Get him off guard, thought Will. Aloud he said, "Getting dark."

"Better get used to it; it's gonna be might dark where you're going," Walker snickered. "Gonna be black."

Get him to relax a bit. "You got the makings?"

"Yeah, but you don't need 'em."

"Every man ought to have his dying wish," Will said. How thick could a man be, he wondered.

"Oh, hell," Walker muttered, fishing in his shirt pocket starting toward Will. His path would take him directly under the twelve-inch supporting beam. "Don't get any funny ideas," he warned.

Trin screamed once, then again. The screams were more in anger than fear, as though she were fighting her assailant savagely, heatedly. Walker stopped. His grin was cruel, like a wild untamed animal.

Come on, Will coaxed him silently. Getchens and Trin must be near the house. Damn you, Walker, just move, Will thought, come on, move.

As if reading his thoughts, Walker glared at Will. But he took a step forward. Then two steps. One more step Will prayed.

Will had been grasping the supporting pole so hard his muscles ached. Every sinew was tightened to the point of ripping fibers. Fibers tuned for maximum response. Just one more step.

As Walker's left foot struck the single board that would put him directly under the beam, Will closed his eyes and . . . unleashed his powerful strength in one smooth, forceful, fluid motion. As he tumbled backwards bringing the support pole with him, he attempted to wedge himself between the bales of pelts for protection. At that same moment, Getchens attempting to open the door to enter the clapboard house turned loose Trin's hair; she brought her head down, and sunk her teeth into his forearm as hard as she possibly could.

Her upper teeth met her lower teeth through the rawhide tough skin. The shriek Getchens emitted was that of a mountain lion caught in a steel-tooth trap. He yanked his arm back before Trin was able to turn loose. He first glared at the bloody torn mess hanging from his forearm, then at Trin's bloody mouth. His expression changed from shocked surprise to that of a raging wild bull. Streams of curses spewed forth as he drew back his balled-up fist.

Trin was saved by the rumbling crash as the roof of the mercantile building disappeared in a cloud of dust.

Getchens turned only to see billowing dust erupt from what had once been the store. Screaming curses with each and every step, he ran toward the collapsing building, Trin forgotten.

By the time Walker look up the large beam was only inches from his face. He had no time to raise his arms for protection before the heavy timber and the loft's floor took him full in the head. His neck was instantly broken. The cocked pistol in his palm exploded. White hot, searing lead ripped through Will's upper left arm.

Rapidly, Will struggled to free himself from beneath the debris which had fallen on him from the loft. The stacks of fur had saved him from serious injury or possibly a crushing death. He kicked away boxes and scraps, wiggling frantically to rid himself from the pole. Blinded by the swirling dust, he fought fiercely to free himself from the wreckage by sliding his arms along the pole to which he was attached.

Finally, free of his burden, he crawled with bound wrists, groping for the shotgun which had been on the bar. But there was no bar. Everything was in shambles. Getchens would be bursting through the door any moment. Near panic, his fingers finally touched the cold steel of the twelve-gauge Greener. His spirits lifted.

Lumbering boots sounded on the porch. There was no time to check to see if it was loaded. Will rolled over, his back to the wall. Thumbing back both hammers, he prayed Getchens hadn't had the sense that God gives a goose to unload the shotgun.

Getchens slammed open the door; in his left hand he held his Navy Colt. "Walker? Walker, what happened?" he shouted, rushing into the room. "Walker, where are . . ." He caught himself looking down the two black holes of the double-barrel Greener. He knew instantly he was staring at death.

"I'm glad you're going to see this." Will squeezed both triggers simultaneously a fraction of a second before Getchens raised his pistol. The blast threw Getchens back through the window, across the porch and into the manure-covered roadway. His body was lifeless before it cleared the window. Will stopped and glanced at Walker's lifeless body. Satisfied, he continued crawling toward the door. Walker was lying on his stomach; head twisted grotesquely, eyes opened wide, never to see again.

Tears of relief filled her eyes as Trin saw Will emerge from what had been the mercantile. Frantically, she ran to meet him. Joyous tears of relief flooded down her blood-stained cheeks. She threw her arms around him.

"Oh, Will. Oh, Will." Tears and laughter were mingled together. "Are they . . . ?"

"They won't be bothering you anymore, or anyone else," he assured her. "Are you okay? Did he . . . your mouth . . ." He noticed the blood around her mouth and cheeks.

"No, he . . . Yes, I'm just fine now," She rubbed the back of her hand across her cheek, mixing tears with dirt and blood. The other hand clutched the torn shirt over her breast. She noticed the blood on his shirt sleeve. "Oh, you're hurt."

"Yeah, and it hurts like hell. But here, help me get these ropes off first," He still held the shotgun. Though empty, it gave him a measure of comfort.

As Trin worked at the ropes, she said, "I've never been so scared. It was horrifying."

His arms now free, Will placed his good arm around Trin's shoulders protectively. She continued to tremble.

"It's going to be all right now, Trin. It's all over," Will stroked her hair gently, "There's nothing to worry about now."

As the trembling subsided somewhat, she began to calm down. "Here, let me see that arm," she said, as she tucked her torn shirt into the top of her trousers to better cover herself.

The arm was going to trouble him a good bit in the near future, but at least there were no torn ligaments. Movement would be restricted somewhat and the pain more of an aggravation than preventive, but Trin was able to stop the bleeding.

"Let's find Booger Red," Will said, sorrow threading his voice.

They found Booger Red in the barn. His feet were tied together, suspended from the rafters upside down over a pool of crimson blood.

"Oh, dear God!" Trin cried mournfully.

As Will work laboriously with one good hand to hold Red up, he directed Trin to loosen the ropes. "Watch his head," Will said as they lowered him slowly to the barn floor.

As Trin knelt beside Booger Red, tears flowed freely and fell onto the viciously beaten form she had come to admire and respect during the short time they had ridden together. She could not forget he had helped to save her life back at the way station.

Will noticed two solid oak singletrees covered with blood, apparently used to batter the life out of his friend. Even though he fought to hold back his emotions welling deep within him, moisture filled his two dark brown eyes. With tightly clenched fist, he knelt beside Booger Red and silently vowed that the remainder of the gang responsible would meet the fate they deserved.

Will joined Trin in the door-way and embraced the grieving girl. Snow-promising clouds obscured the mountains in the distance. The cold air only served to tighten the sharp bond of pain for both Will and Trin.

SIX

At first Will thought it was the wail of the chilling wind. He whirled around as the sound reached his ears again, and he ran to Booger Red's side.

"What is it?" Trin asked.

"He's alive!" Will shouted. "Get a bucket of water from the trough. Hurry!"

Through the long cold night that followed, Will remained by the side of his companion. Only once did he leave Trin alone with the injured man; when he went to scrounge for provisions, blankets and a shirt for Trin.

Trin proved to be a competent nurse. She insisted Booger Red not be moved. If their suspicion of broken ribs was true, there was a real danger of puncturing a lung.

*   *   *

Try as she might, Trin couldn't keep her eyes open. She awoke with a snap, suddenly aware of Will's absence; she started to panic, but sighed with great relief as Will strolled through the door with his arms loaded. Surprisingly, he had a pot of coffee.

"Getting light out," Will offering her a cup of coffee. "He seems to be resting comfortably."

"Thanks," she said accepting the coffee. "What are we going to do, Will?"

"There's an old wagon out back. I may be able to do something with it, at least good enough to get him to a doctor in Trinidad." He looked over at Red. "Horseback is definitely out of the question."

Trin nodded. In a low voice, she said, "Yes, he needs a doctor badly. I was only able to set his broken arm, temporarily of course. I think it was only a light fracture, nothing serious. But he's lost a lot of blood, and there is no way we can know how bad he's hurt inside." Her weighty concern was evident as her voice broke, "I'm so sorry, Will."

"There's no need for you to feel sorry, Trin. You've done all you could and been very courageous," Will assured her. "We're mighty indebted to you; I don't know what I'd've done without your help. I'll tell you something else, too. My brother is one lucky man. I know he cares a lot for you, and he couldn't have chosen a better lady than you."

Trin's face flushed bright pink. "Thank you, Will. But I'm the lucky one. Your brother is a wonderful man."

She stood, pulled the blanket around her shoulders, and said, "I'll be back in a minute."

Sounding much like an older brother, Will said, "Where are you going?"

"Will!" she said, smiling through a renewed blush, "a woman needs a have a little privacy once in a while, you know."

"Oh, sorry," Will mumbled, embarrassed and mentally kicking himself for acting like a back-country oaf. He just hoped she hadn't seen the red flush he felt heating his face.

Later, Trin was able to coax Booger Red to drink a cup of broth she had made with some dried beef Will had found. She had forgotten how ravenously hungry she had become until she was preparing slab bacon and pan-fried bread for Will and herself. She knew Will was in the same shape when the sound of his growling stomach reached her ears as she handed him a well-laden plate.

After they satisfied their hunger and finished their third cup of coffee, Trin said, "Will, I don't mean to pry where it's none of my business, but that man with the pocked-marked face, Elkhart, I believe you called him; well, he scares me."

"You've nothing to be afraid of, Trin," he assured her. "It's me he wants."

"You want to talk about it?"

"Not much to tell really," Will said. "He was the sergeant in charge of the guards at Marysville where I spent the latter part of the war. He's the most vicious, brutal and merciless man I've ever come across. He beat prisoners within an inch of their lives. I think just because he enjoyed it. Some died as the direct result of his constant torture. Even the commander of the camp feared him.

"Shortly before we were released, we received a new camp commander. It didn't take long for him to catch on to Sergeant Elkhart's brutality. One day after Elkhart had been called on the carpet, so to speak, he sought me out. He was the man in charge of interrogations, and he hadn't been able to break me, and it infuriated the man. He was so damn crazed he couldn't think straight. Later that day, he attacked me during roll-call for no other reason than to show-off in front of the commander. Well, I darn near killed the man. God knows I wanted to. The commander saw the fight, but refused to stop it. I never saw Elkhart again until yesterday. There were rumors he was kicked out, or rather, cashiered out of the Army. One of the guards told me when I was released that Elkhart blamed me for his downfall, and would be waiting for me when I got out."

"He'll try to kill you, won't he?"

"He'll try. He's not one to forget," Will declared. "I doubt very seriously if he knew Colonel Bullard's instructions to Walker and Getchens to have you and me eliminated. He would want that pleasure himself."

Will drained the last of his coffee. "I'll get started on the wagon, and see what I can work out."

Trin had just knelt to check Booger Red when suddenly her head snapped up. "Someone's coming, Will."

He, too, heard the sound of riders approaching. His first thought was Bullard and his gangs were returning to see if his instructions had been carried out. He grabbed up the shotgun, along with a rifle he had taken from the wrecked store, and checking the loads, hurried to the front of the barn, "Stay with Booger Red and stay out of sight, no matter what happens," he ordered Trin.

Will stepped out into the road, levering a cartridge into the Winchester .44. Although he couldn't see the oncoming horsemen, the drumming of hooves was unmistakable; there were six or seven riders.

Overhead, the threatening clouds were drifting slowly eastward. Occasionally, snowflakes had been just fluttering softly to the ground; now it was beginning to snow much harder. The air had the smell of a heavy snow-fall. Marshal Langley had apparently been correct in his predication of a harsh winter storm. A serious early winter storm in these mountains was not to Will's liking. Dain and his father were somewhere in those mountains, and searching for them could be mighty difficult with a heavy snow.

As the riders came into view, Will was relieved to see they were strangers; still, he couldn't take chances. Caution was necessary in these parts. His concern at the moment was for Booger Red and Trin. He had made one dire mistake when he led his companions into a trap the day before, and he would not let himself become so careless again. He held his rifle with his finger on the trigger.

The group of riders slowed, then came to a halt still some distance from Will. They saw Getchens's body laying in the dust, and the destroyed mercantile building; and then all the dark eyes turned toward Will.

Will had heard stories of the Mexicans, but never had an opportunity dealing with them. But he knew this group of Mexicans was not to be taken lightly. One thing for sure, they were loaded for bear. Many of them held a rifle across his saddle. Most had at least one pistol, and possibly two with numerous knives visible everywhere.

Dark eyes peered under wide-brimmed, flat-crowned hats. "What has happened, Senor? And who, may I ask, are you?" The speaker wore a well-trimmed mustache over a grim, determined mouth. There was no smile.

"Who's asking?" Will stood firm.

"Amigo," he began, crossing his arms over the oversized Mexican horn, "You are only one, but we are many, eh? Besides, we have many friends here. We would be most upset if harm should befall them."

Pete and Fran had been friends of theirs?

"That being the case, I'm afraid I have some bad news for you," Will watched carefully for their reactions.

"What is it you have to tell us, Senor?" The voice was soft, yet firm, authoritative.

Then Will saw her. She had kneed the powerful black stallion forward. Will was looking into the darkest, most beautiful eyes he had ever seen. Her coal black hair was tied at the nape, the tips of which hung down to touch the cantle of her saddle. He had seen beautiful women, but none to compare to her. It never occurred to him that any one person could be so breathtaking beautiful.

Realizing he was holding his breath, his heart fluttered as he answered haltingly, "I'm sorry, but I'm afraid that Pete and Fran are both dead."

The only change in her uncompromising expression was that of swift pain. Tension filled the air, pistols cocked. Will waited.

"You have done this thing, Senor?" the lady asked, steel threaded her voice.

"No. I did not," Will stated, meeting her gaze steadfastly.

"Juanita! Pico!" Trin said, racing from the barn. "Oh, I'm so glad you're here."

"Trin? What are you doing in Ludlow?" The lady, Juanita, asked in shocked surprised. She hurriedly dismounted and ran to embrace Trin. "Is it true? Pete and Fran are dead? Were they killed? What happened?"

"Yes, Juanita. I'm afraid it's true. I'll tell you about it later, but right now we need your help." She touched Will's arm. "We have a badly injured man in the barn. Come. Please?"

Juanita followed Trin into the barn. The fragrance of her as she brushed by him teased Will's natural senses. She returned shortly, and in Spanish, began calling names, giving directions, and pointing toward the house, and the collapsed mercantile. The men broke in every direction, leaving Will alone, confused, and forgotten. He turned to enter the barn to see what was going on, but she blocked his path, her hands on her hips. Her stance was firm, but the smile she gave him was gentle. "Stay, Senor. Juan will do everything that can be done for now. He is very good with these things."

Feeling useless, Will retreated to sit on the porch of the wrecked store.

One of the Mexican riders, who had accompanied Juanita and Trin, returned and introduced himself. "They call me Pico, Senor. I think it would be best if we got under the porch, and out of the snow. Juan will be a long time, I think."

Will recognized him as the man who rode to the right side of Juanita. Will had not realized until now he would protect his senorita with his life. He would stick to Will like glue until he was sure he could be trusted.

"It is a brave thing you have done for the Senorita Trin,"

"It was no more than any other man would have done," Will replied. He looked into the friendly, smiling expression of the Mexican.

"No, Senor," he responded, offering Will a long slender cigar. "No, not any man. Those two hombres much bad, I think."

Will shrugged and accepted the offering. "Not any more they ain't," he said.

"Si, Senor," Pico laughed, revealing gleaming white teeth. "Senorita Trin, she tells everything, I think. Your brother, he is taken by the bad men to your papa, eh? Senor Bucklett is one fine hombre. I think."

"You know my pa?" Will asked in surprise.

"Si, he is amigo to all Maestas's hacienda for long time," Pico answer seriously.

Will nodded his head in response. He looked at Pico speculatively for a moment. "Could you tell me about the lay of the land up ahead?"

"Si, Senor," Pico answered without hesitation. "Pico, he knows the mountains very well. I would be pleased and honored to assist you."

"This is something I have to do on my own," Will said. "If you could sort of draw me a map of how these mountains lay, I'd be much obliged."

Will knew the map Pico sketched out for him would prove a valuable tool in his search for locating Dain and his father. He expressed his thanks to Pico. He was torn between his responsibility to Booger Red, Trin and the situation here in Ludlow, but the need to be on the trail in his search was great. But he realized he must soon be on his way before the snow covered all traces of a trail.

The bodies of Pete and Fran lay covered in the bed of the wagon the Mexican had repaired. Walker and Getchens's bodies had long since been removed. Booger Red, lying on an improvised stretcher, was being loaded onto the wagon.

Pico and Will watched Trin and Juanita approach. Will's gaze locked with Juanita's with an intensity that surprised him.

"Juan says he has a very good chance," Trin said, speaking of Booger Red. "Besides the broken arm, three fingers are smashed, and it's possible he might have one or two cracked ribs." She paused. "Thank God; Juan says he is fairly sure there is no internal bleeding. He says Red will be laid up for a while, but he should be good as new in time."

"Is this Juan a doctor?" Will asked.

"Si, Senor," Pico declared. "The Maestas's ranch has the best horses in all of Colorado. Do not worry, he is the best."

"You mean he's a horse doctor?" Will demanded.

"A doctor is a doctor, no?" Pico expressed, surprised at Will's reaction.

"Senor Bucklett," Juanita stated coolly, "there is no need for you to be overly concerned. I can assure you Juan is very competent. He has been with our family for many years."

Will turned to his friend lying in the wagon. His concerns and worry were apparent for all to see. Juan, seeing his distress, said, "He is very strong, Senor. I will take very good care of your friend. You must trust me."

Juanita began talking to Pico in rapid Spanish. It was obvious they weren't in agreement. Hot words flowed swiftly back and forth at an alarming rate. Trin turned to Will, "Pico is upset. Juanita wants to return to the ranch. They were escorting her to Trinidad to visit her aunt. Pico is saying Don Maestas will have his head if his wishes are not carried out. But, Juanita is firm about postponing the trip to Trinidad." Pico, obviously overruled, threw up his hand, and started barking orders to the men.

Juanita turned to Will and Trin, "We are returning to the hacienda. It is best your friend have the best of care. You will, of course, return with us," she stated.

Will wasn't sure if she was commanding or requesting their company. There was nothing he would like better at the present than to share some time with this lovely creature, to become better acquainted, but it just couldn't be. "I appreciate your offer, ma'am," he told her, "but I've got other things to do, as you well know."

Juanita regarded him with skepticism, "But you must come with us. You are wounded and must be cared for also."

"My family is in need of my help," Will maintained. "I'm obliged to you for looking after Booger Red and Trin. I'm in your debt."

"I do not do it for your indebtness, Senor Bucklett," she informed him firmly.

Will was astonished by the fire in her eyes. He was immediately sorry for the unintended affront.

"No offense meant, ma 'am," Will offered an apology. "But I have to do what I have to do."

"Then I will send men with you," Juanita insisted.

Trin, listening closely, smiled, aware of the magnetic vibrations between her two friends.

"No. I'll travel alone," Will asserted. "I don't want to be responsible for anyone else getting hurt. There's been too much bloodshed already."

"This is absurd," Juanita said fiercely. "You will be killed. They are many. You are only one."

"Seems like I've heard that before," Will countered lightly.

Juanita twirled around and marched swiftly away, back straight, head held high, anger in each eye.

Trin and Pico were both grinning, amused at the heated exchange between Will and Juanita. They wondered at the prospects of future developments between the two self-willed people. Pico looked at Will with deep admiration. No man had ever bested Juanita in a contest of wills.

Will shrugged, "It appears that woman has been accustomed to having everything her way."

"Si, Senor. That is true," Pico chuckled, relishing the brief confrontation. "Don Maestas will be surprised, as I am, to know she has met a man who will stand up to her."

"Senor Bucklett?" Juanita suddenly returned, leading the fine black stallion she had ridden on when they arrived. "Are you so proud you will not accept the finest mountain horse of the Maestas stock, or are you going to be stubborn about that as well?" she challenged. Not waiting for Will's shock to subside, she shoved the reins in his hand. She turned to leave, but not before her dark eyes darted toward Pico, daring him to protest.

"Come, Trin. Pico, we must go now," she said, commandingly.

Trin hugged Will tightly, and kissed his cheek. "We'll be waiting at the Maestas ranch. Be careful and tell Dain . . . ." She could say no more, but Will understood.

Will assisted Trin up to the wagon to sit beside Juanita, who kept her head erect, facing forward. Will felt somewhat depressed that Juanita and he were not departing on better terms, yet he was at a loss for words. The black-haired beauty left him confused and greatly puzzled. He would have been more bewildered if he had been able to read her thoughts.

Standing alone in the middle of the road, he looked at the large, powerful black stallion. It crossed his mind how much the beast reminded him of its owner's stunning beauty. "Now, I guess you're going to try and tell me what I should do, right?"

The black nodded his head vigorously, blowing forcefully.

"I thought so," Will laughed, shaking his head. "Well, horse, let's see if you're as good as you look."

The stallion was more than ready to travel. Will decided to let him have his head. The horse and rider preformed like a well-oiled machine. They hit the mouth of Beer Canyon with the black going flat out. As he hauled back on the reins, the black fought him; he hadn't had enough; he wanted to run. Will stroked and patted the strong, sleek neck, "Save it, fella, we may need that energy later on," he told the horse soothingly.

According to the tracks Will found in the sandy bottom of Beer Canyon, Colonel Bullard, Dain, and the two gunmen were traveling at a fast clip. He traveled well into the night, at times by the light of a cupped sulfur match. Having no idea of their destination, he only knew he didn't want to inadvertently stumble onto their camp, if indeed they had stopped for the night. He would just be happy for them to lead him to his pa. Then, with a little thinking and a whole lot of luck, maybe he could somehow . . . . Well, there was no need to dwell on it now, he thought. Best open the door before he tried to get the horses out.

The clouds above finally blanketed the scant starlight. Darkness settled on him in the blink of an eye. Although it had stopped snowing, what lay on the ground reflected enough light to give him sure footing. Bowing to the inevitable and gathering a handful of twigs, he had a small blaze going in a matter of minutes.

After pulling off his saddle and giving the horse a good rub down, he put a few oats he had thought to bring from Ludlow in his hat for the black. With the horse taken care of, he set about taking care of his own grumbling stomach. With the coffee boiling, he liked it black and strong, he knifed open a can of tomatoes and dug out an old cold biscuit from his saddle bags he had brought from Tascosa.

Later, enjoying the last of the coffee and the long thin cigar Pico had given him, he turned his thoughts to ponder the last few days. He found that thinking was useless, for a picture of Juanita kept floating before his eyes, interfering with his thoughts. So much had happened these past few weeks, it was nearly impossible to sort things out. There were so many questions to be answered. Everything seemed to be all jumbled up together. Where did it all start? Where does it end?

Was there a missing gold shipment? Bullard seemed sincere, very adamant about it being a fact. Was Pa involved? What was Elkhart's play in all this? How had he gotten tied up with Bullard? The woman, Evie, and her brother, Tobe—where did they fit in to all this? Or did they? Could Salas explain everything? But where was he? Where was Dain? Were they both okay?

Turning onto his right side to ease the ache in his left arm, Will pulled the blanket around his shoulders and tried to erase the worry from his mind, leaving the black to warn him of any danger.

SEVEN

Will scratched away the partially burned tender of the dead campfire. Below the cold ashes the ground still held some degree of warmth, more than he had found at the camp-site earlier in the day. Although they were a good distance ahead of him, his spirits lifted with the knowledge that he was making headway in closing the gap between them.

He felt he had the advantage for two reasons. First, they were not aware he was behind them. Therefore, the colonel not sensing there was any danger from Will, would feel no need to rush. In fact, he may begin to feel more relaxed and over-confident in his mission. Secondly, he was astride the powerful black stallion. Their mounts may be mountain wise, but their horses would lack the strength and endurance to compete with the masterful piece of horseflesh Juanita had so graciously placed in his hands. The stallion took to the high country and Will's weight as if he was going downhill with a feather on his back.

Swing back into the saddle, Will looked toward the boulder blanketed prominence waiting to be ascended. Clucking the black into motion and knowing that it would have taken the colonel and his party some measure of time to climb the grade, he smiled. "Come on, horse," he said.

Will had been traveling west and north most of the day. The colonel made little, if any, attempt to disguise their tracks or the direction of travel. They were making a beeline to their destination, when not deterred by difficult terrain. Will was being led through rock strewn draws, canyons, and dry washes. Studying the map Pico had drawn, he believed he would be able to take another route and come out ahead of the colonel. Or at the very least make up a lot of travel time.

Swinging back into the saddle, he looked toward the boulder-blanketed prominence waiting to be ascended. He chucked the black into motion, knowing would take the colonel and his party a good measure of time to climb the grade. He padded the strong muscular neck, "Let's show 'em how it's done; earn yourself an extra portion of oats." He reined the horse in a new direction.

As if to answer his rider, the stallion jumped toward the steep, jagged landscape. If Will hadn't known better, he would have suspected that at the pinnacle a mare in her rutting stage awaited the magnificent.

Will glanced skyward as he rode along the ridge overlooking a lush, fertile valley. A shear drop of over two hundred feet trailed along on his left. Luckily, so far, the storm had held its threatening pose in check. Nightfall was coming on fast and to be caught on an open plateau at this altitude was not in the best position being in. It was imperative for him to find a trail leading to the valley below.

Will rode another half hour before it became necessary for him to call a halt for the night. The chance of bypassing a trail to the bottom was too great. He saw no alternative except to spend the night on the open plateau, but the menace of unfavorable weather conditions weighed heavily on his mind. He thought he glimpsed something afar off from the corner of his eye as he started to reins the black around. Quickly, he looked back. What could it have been? Was it a flicker of light of a campfire? Just my imagination running away with me, he thought. The light was fading too rapidly; he turned back to loosen the cinch. He blinked and rubbed his eyes. He searched again, no movement, nothing.

He began to think his fatigue was playing with his imagination, when suddenly he saw it again. Yes, just the smallest twinkle of light from a campfire, afar off up the valley. It could be two miles or twenty. At this altitude the air was so transparent; judging distances was a guessing game. He was thankful now that he had decided to camp here on this high plateau. Had he not been this high above the valley, he doubted if he would have seen the glimmer of light. Though somewhat elated, he rejected the idea of getting any closer tonight. Just the scent of the black by one of their mounts would undoubtedly alert the colonel of unwanted company.

"Horse," Will said, grinning widely, "you deserve and extra portion of oats tonight."

Will pulled back off the skyline, and found a small depression surrounded by enough cedar and brush oak to provide adequate cover and concealment. He gathered a few twigs for a small fire to boil of water for a cup or two of coffee.

Anticipating a longer wait for the coffee to boil because of the high altitude, he gave the black a lengthy rub-down amid murmured words of appreciation for its participation in the day's grueling pace.

When the horse was munching contently on the promised oats, Will, coffee in hand, walked back up to the top of the ridge to check on the light he had seen. Leaning on a large boulder, he pondered what may lie before him. As he chewed on the last of his hard tack and sipped the steaming, syrup-like, thick brew, he thought of a thick steak, fried potatoes, fresh apple pie, and fresh, spring-cooled milk.

Will had his last cup of cold coffee, and was in the saddle long before false dawn broke in the east. He'd taken a last bead on the position of the campfire he had observed before tossing out the coffee grounds and swinging into the saddle.

The sky was laced with mare's tail here and there, but toward the north, high billowing, dark clouds promised a quick change in the weather. The temperature had dropped drastically during the night, and Will knew the snow that had been threatening would not be delayed much longer.

Upon reaching the valley, Will found out Bullard had begun taking various precautions to cover their trail. If he hadn't notice their campfire the night before, he might have ridden by it unsuspectingly. They had taken some pains to brush out their tracks, but to a mountain-wise tracker, they came up short of having good sense. They left a clearer trace in trying to wipe out their tracks than what they intended to accomplish. Will circled the camp, taking his time to find what he was looking for: a sign of some sort left by Dain. There it was: stones in the shape of an arrow. Yet, it appeared in a natural array to the untrained eye. The arrow indicated the party would be proceeding to the northwest. Three overturned smaller stones in front of the arrow told Will they would be changing directions. If the three stones had been in the vertex of the arrow, they would be continuing in their present direction of travel. Yet, they were changing directions. Had they spotted him? It wasn't likely. Dain would have warned him some way. Just in case, he would have to be a little more cautious. The three overturned stones also noted that Dain believed they were three days ride from their intended destination.

Will was not surprised that Dain had been able to leave the silent message. No doubt about it, thought Will, Dain was a smart, cunning man; and he was mighty proud to call him his brother.

They were now watching their back trail. About midday, Will found where one man had held to timber, and had evidently watched their back trail for some time. They were also taking care to cross on rocky ground and keeping to the underbrush, leaving minimum clues of their passing.

The trouble they were taking was soon of little consequence. It started snowing, not hard, just large fluffy flakes here and there, floating lazily down to gently, embellishing the landscape. Hoping it would blow over, Will maintained his pace.

With hope-shattering speed, suddenly the clouds dumped the promised abundance. In an amazing short time, the ground was covered and visibility was nonexistent.

For two full days, Will lived under a giant deadfall which lay against a boulder the size of a small house. The natural cavern was sufficient protection from the elements for both man and beast. To venture out into the blinding snow-storm was impossible. At times it became a complete whiteout. He would become lost in a matter of seconds, unable to return to the shelter he now enjoyed. There was sufficient food for him and the horse, and branches from the fallen tree provided adequate fuel for a small fire.

By the time the storm broke, he was getting low on coffee, water, and oats. The storm ceased as it had begun—suddenly. The sun's brilliant rays smashed the virgin blanket with a blinding force. Following the colonel and Dain was out of the question. All evidence that the foursome ever existed had been wiped out by the storm.

Pulling out the roughly drawn map Pico had provided, Will attempted to orientate his position using available landmarks he was able to see from his present location.

He knew one thing for sure; his travel put him left of Spanish Peaks. Tracing where he entered Beer Canyon after leaving Ludlow, he had taken the right fork up Stock Canyon, crossed some rolling hills and ridges covered with pinion, junipers and scattered blue spruce pine. Judging from the crude map, his refuge from the storm would have to have been in the Wildcat Creek area. That being the case, he would be due north and about a good day's ride in good weather from the Maestas Ranch.

He had two choices; first, keep traveling in the direction he believed the colonel and his party were journeying; or, secondly, make for the Maestas Ranch and seek assistance. That thought didn't sit too well with him; besides, going back to the ranch would delay him at least one, but most likely, two full precious days. The thought of seeing Juanita again was tempting, but completely out of the question. Two days could possibly mean the difference between life and death to either Dain or Pa, if not both. So, Will thought, there was really no choice to make. He pushed on.

With the exception of the comfortable rub of saddle leather and the muffled sound of the stallion's hooves in the deep, powdery snow, there was absolutely no other noise; no birds chirping, no wind singing in the tall pine, just peaceful, soul-pleasing silence.

Will gained about a thousand feet in altitude, going up the valley since the snowing stopped. Clouds were again beginning to form over the three sharp peaks which lay off to his right. According to the sketch in his pocket, the three peaks were the North, Middle, and Middle White Peak Range. Off to his left stood Parks Mountain, over ten-thousand feet in height. The saddle pass between them was nearly as steep as the mountains themselves. With no way to go except up, it was going to prove to be mighty tough going, even for the formidable black.

He broke into a clearing at the top of the saddle just west of the base of Middle White Peak. The clearing was about ten acres and oval in shape, just the place for a breather, giving the black a short rest.

Will had no more than remounted when the black's ears came up and forward in a sign of warning. Across the opening a party of Indians broke from the tree line—six warriors riding in single file. There were two deer carcasses hanging from two of the ponies. A hunting party was Will's first thought. In the stillness he could hear them talking, bantering back and forth. They were, at the present, unaware of his presence.

They continued to proceed along the edge of the tree line; then crossing in front of Will, they went from left to right. Will had his hand over the black's muzzle; otherwise he dared not move a muscle or make a sound. Only a few snow-cover pine branches stood between him and the frolicking Indian braves. However, if any one of them happened to glance his way, there was no doubt in his mind that he wouldn't be noticed. With the near solid white background of snow, the great black horse would stand out like a piss hole in a snow bank. Seconds passed away so excruciatingly and slowly. Will began to relax as the leader turned, at last, into the distant grove of aspens. When the last man following turned into the trees, the Indian preceding him released a heavy branch, which sprang back, knocking the young brave topsy-turvy over his horse's rump. The brave jumped up brushing snow off amid the joshing and good-humored teasing. His movements were halted suddenly as his eyes settled on Will and the great black horse.

"Aieeee." The deep-throated, spine-curling war cry sent a chill shuddering down Will's back-bone. The young brave caught up his spear and vaulted effortlessly onto the standing pony. Before any of his companions knew what was happening, the brave was half-way across the clearing, hell bent toward Will, shrieking at the top of his lungs.

Blue Wolf, in his fifteenth winter, wanted badly to prove himself to the other older warriors. He made no kill on the hunt, hadn't even come close. He was exhilarated to have the chance to redeem himself, to count coup on the white man. He thanked his Wolf Spirit for providing him the white stranger, for he would surely be welcomed into Lightning Bear's Black Arrow Society. Yes, his Wolf Spirit was good to him, he thought. So overcome with joy and thankfulness he did not feel some unseen object slam into his body. His vision blurred, wondering why he was lying in the cold, wet snow. Blue Wolf was unable to hear his comrades' pick up the war cry as his spirit welcomed the engulfing darkness.

The black stallion stood firm as Will levered two more quick shots into the approaching Indians. The leader went head over heels as his horse went tumbling in the snow. A second brave flung his arms skyward as a .44 smacked his shoulder, slamming him to the ground. The others pulled up, milling around, trying to decide if the single white man was worth the risk.

Will decided not to wait around to witness their conclusion. He dug his heels into the black's flanks. The stallion propelled himself into a motion which almost unseated the rider. To go back the way he had come would be most certainly inviting death. The remaining braves would be breathing down his neck before he could get fifty yards. He trusted the black, but could the beast out-run the Indian ponies in such rough terrain? Will needed open country and soon.

Across the clearing and off to his left lay an opening in the dense thicket Will had marked in his mind earlier. He nudged the black toward the opening with his knees; the horse hit the opening, nostrils flared, his ears laid back. Hearing whoops and shouts Will turned in the saddle, and threw a couple of ineffective shots in the general direction of the pack behind him. The lead Indians was well out in front of his other companions, closing the distance between them dangerously close. Two arrows swished within inches of Will's head, falling harmlessly to the ground in his path. Suddenly, he felt a hot sting in his right shoulder, and knew he had taken an arrow. Will put his hand under his right arm and felt where the sharp point of the arrow punctured through his shirt and skin. He brought his hand away sticky with blood.

They were now racing down a long low area between hills laced intermittently with beaver ponds, both sides thick with frost-bitten aspen, and too close together to get through. Eyes watering from the cold, stinging wind, he saw a way out at the end of the long, sloping meadow. The blue of a distant mountain range through the trees ahead was a welcomed sight.

Will knew the thin atmosphere of the high altitude was causing the stallion problems. He began laboring, sucking in great gulps of air that just wasn't there. Will feared the already tired horse wouldn't last much longer. Yet, as the rider spoke encouragement, the magnificent beast found renewed strength.

Will was well out in front and out of range of the Indians when their ponies began to falter. As he came to the opening at the end of the meadow, his hope was reawakened: before him lay an open downgrade. Neither the black nor Will saw the snow-covered log. Suddenly, Will went head over teakettle, flying over the stallion's head.

The pain was excruciating as the impact broke the arrow shaft projecting from his back. Stunned from the pain and the intense jolt, he crawled toward the log which had caused his fall. His rifle was gone, lying somewhere in the deep snow. The stallion, unharmed, ran off down the mountain. Will thumbed back the hammer of the revolver, and placed the barrel across the log. From ten feet away, Will's first shot blew the Indian from his horse. The bare-chested brave kicked in agony a few times, and then went still. The remaining two Indians skid their ponies to a halt some distance back, out of revolver range. Shouting, waving their arms, and making obscene gestures as they disappeared into the tree line. They had little desire to follow their companions to the land beyond the sun.

Suddenly, it was over; only the cold, the stillness and the pain remained. The gripping, wet coldness began to soak through Will's clothing. The only warmth he felt was his own blood seeping from the sharp pain in his shoulder.

Will grasped the protruding arrowhead firmly, ground his teeth together, took a deep breath, and yanked it forward and out. He was unable to combat the dark haven that offered a welcome release. He fell forward, his right shoulder pressing against the frigid moisture.

*   *   *

Pico and Miguel were beating the brush for Maestas's cattle in the breaks off Sawtooth Rock. The early storm made it necessary to drive the stranded cattle to the more protected lower pastures. Hearing gunfire in the distance, Pico's first thought was a couple of his men had run into a party of Utes or Cheyenne. He and Miguel didn't slow their mounts until they approached the clearing where Will had encountered the Indians. Knowing caution was necessary, they carefully scanned the area before entering the clearing. Only one body was visible—no horse, no Indians. Slowly, they approached the snow-covered body, guns drawn and ready.

Pico's sharply indrawn breath marked his recognition of Will.

"Senor Bucklett?" Miguel asked in stark surprise. "Is he dead?"

Pico knelt and gently examined Will. "No, amigo," he answered. "Not yet. He has lost much blood. If this man does not live, our Senorita Juanita will be very deep in sorrow, I think."

EIGHT

If Dain had ever been colder, his memory failed to pin-point the time. The wind blowing down from the high mountain peaks penetrated his clothing like tiny, needle-like icicles. His ears and nose had long been numb from the freezing temperature they had experienced since early morning.

His hands, a bluish purple, were tied to the saddle horn. With difficulty he managed to rub them together, hoping to prevent frostbite. His feet were so deadened with the bitter cold, he couldn't have sworn if his boots where on his feet or not. Whenever he was able to move one of his limbs, it felt as if sharp needles raced through them. He had seen men lose toes and fingers from frostbite, and knew without better circulation soon it was possible he would suffer the same fate.

In an effort to direct his thoughts elsewhere, Dain remembered the miserable, intolerable long days they had waited out the sudden snow-storm. Immediately after the storm passed, they were in the saddle again and on their way. They'd been in the saddle for only a few short hours, when Bullard and Elkhart got into a very heated argument. He hadn't been able to hear the exchange, but it was obvious Bullard won out. Elkhart took off riding up a canyon off their flank.

Bullard had then turned to Skeets, "I'll keep an eye on Dain. You get a fire going and put on the coffee pot."

"Where's Elkhart going?" Skeets asked.

"None of your damn business," Bullard answered sarcastically.

Skeets shrugged and started to untie Dain's hands from the saddle horn, but the colonel stopped him short.

"Leave him be," he directed.

"You want him to freeze to death? That's fine with me. No skin off my nose," Skeets countered.

"Just leave him be. I give the orders here, and whatever I say goes." His eyes were hard on Skeets. "You'd do well to remember that."

As soon as Skeets left to gather fire-wood, Bullard untied Dain's hands, and helped him to the ground. Leading him to a nearby tree, he warned, "If you know what's good for you, you'll stay right here."

"Tying me up is really not necessary; I'm sticking to you like glue, at least until I see pa." Dain assured Bullard.

Dain watched as the two men squatted near the fire, wondering how one person could possibly be so utterly inhuman. The kind of treatment he had been receiving caused a deep worry about his father. How much had his pa been forced to endure?

Bullard walked over to Dain, holding a steaming cup of coffee under Dain's nose. "Hot, too. It warms a man all the way down." His grin was malicious as he turned back to the glowing fire.

"You think that was necessary?" Skeets asked.

Skeets's question was rewarded with a swift, hard kick to the ribs. Bullard's curses rained down on Skeets with utter insanity. With his pistol drawn and cocked, Bullard aimed another boot toward Skeet's head. Skeets avoided having his head removed by ducking aside only to have the heavy boot slam into his shoulder. Red hot embers scattered as Skeets rolled across the campfire. Skeets leaped up shaking his head, reaching for his gun, livid with the thought of killing Bullard. Only his quick sense of survival saved him from certain death as he looked into the large bore of Bullard's pistol. Suddenly, the fight went out of Skeets. Skeets glanced feebly back at Dain. To Dain, the glance was a look of apology before he lowered his eyes. But Dain knew if push came to shove, he could not expect any assistance or help in any way from Skeets. Self-preservation would, of course, win out over any pity he may feel for Dain.

Dain's gaze turned again to Bullard. Chills prickled Dain's scalp. He saw in that instant that Bullard was more than sadistic: the man was insane. He was strutting around the campfire holding his cup as if it was a scepter, gesturing wildly, spilling coffee, completely unaware of the spectacle he presented. He appeared to be singularly engrossed in the lecture he was now delivering to Skeets.

"Get one thing straight, Skeets. It's quite obvious that you are sadly lacking the glorious experience of military training; therefore, I'll overlook your ignorant, insubordinate outburst this one time. I'm in charge here, your commanding officer. You work for me, and don't you forget it. This mission is dependent on every order being obeyed to the infinite degree. When I give an order, I mean for it to be carried out to the letter." He paused and stared hard at Dain. "Bucklett stays tied, and he only gets what I say he gets. I don't care if he did promise he wouldn't try to escape. I don't trust him. I want him prepared for what's in store for him. He must be prepared to accomplish his task as I have instructed. If he doesn't cooperate when he sees his father, then he must suffer the consequences."

Dain knew better than to open his mouth at this point, but he had tried and continued to try to convince Bullard that tied or untied there was no way he wanted to get away from Bullard. Every mile he traveled with Bullard was a mile closer to his father.

Elkhart returned from his ride up the canyon and took the lead after some heated discussion over how to proceed.

On the western slope of the Sangre de Cristos, the four made their way cautiously down Wagon Creek Canyon. Strewn with boulders and deadfalls, it was hazardous going. It was getting late in the afternoon when they emerged abruptly into a large valley. High peaks on either side of the long green valley protected the sparsely dotted meadows with pockets of young aspen and a few scattered pines. A clear, snow-melting river meandering through the valley, laced intermittently with a few cottonwood and elm.

Dain saw immediately the reason it was protected from the terrible northern weather. It was sheltered on three sides by giant, towering peaks of mountain ranges. It was open only to the southwest as far as the eyes could see. It sat at the bottom of a natural "S" formed by Lindsey Mountain and the San Isabel Mountain Range, a smaller range of the Sangre de Cristos.

The colonel pulled to a halt. "Elkhart put a blindfold on Bucklett."

"I'll do it," Skeets offered, riding up from Dain's rear. Dain sensed Skeets went to some trouble to make sure the bandana served to protect his nose and ears as much as possible from the cold.

Again they started out; Elkhart led them off in a large circle, and then struck off to the north. If he thought he was confusing Dain, he was badly mistaken. Before Skeets blindfolded him, he felt the wind hit him sharply on the right side. Now they were traveling directly into the bitter cold breeze. He also notice a small plume of smoke a good distance up the valley coming off the eastern slope of Mount Lindsey. He figured it was a good bet they were headed for the column of smoke.

The warmth of the cabin hit Dain like a sledge-hammer as he was pushed through the door. It was hard for him to concentrate on anything except the tingling pains stabbing through his limbs as the heat began to penetrate his body.

The scent of freshly cooked food and hot coffee brought forth a loud grumbling from his stomach. He was so hungry, he felt nauseated and weak. With the exception of a small sip of water, he had had nothing to eat in the past three days.

"What took you so long? You've been gone for over a week." The voice was deep and harsh, but unmistakingly that of a woman.

"We got caught up in the blizzard and had to lay up for a while," the Colonel answered irritably. "Where's Tobe?"

"He went out to see if he could kill a deer or something; we're nearly out of meat," the woman replied.

"Damn it, Evie! I told you I didn't want either one of you leaving this cabin," Bullard yelled. "Besides, he couldn't hit the broad-side of a barn with his nose stuck in a crack. He'll likely do us all a favor and freeze to death." Turning to Skeets he ordered, "Skeets, go out and see if you can find that idiot."

Bullard turned back to Evie, "What about Bucklett?"

"Salas is in pretty bad shape," Evie said nonchalantly. "It's a wonder he's lasted this long. I suggest if you want to find out where that gold is, you'd best get him to talk before you have to bury the old man," she paused. "Which one is this?" she asked approaching Dain.

"The young one, Dain," Bullard said removing the blindfold. "So you didn't have any luck getting the old man to talk like you were bragging you could?"

"Where is Pa? I swear, if you've harmed him in any way, you'll regret it until the day you die."

"So, you're Salas's youngest offspring he sired from that bitch," her expression was a mask of hatred. Sneering, she continued, "Your pa's through that door there. He's sick and he may die, but I don't give a damn one way or the other. But what happens now is up to you."

"Just let me see Pa," Dain said flatly.

Evie's face was somewhat familiar, but it only took a moment for Dain to remember where he had seen her. The day before his mother took seriously ill, he had escorted her to Hot Springs for shopping and a few supplies. After loading the supplies, he had gone to the Spring Water Café to meet his mother for lunch before returning to Mount Ida. As he was entering the restaurant, he inadvertently bumped in to lady in her rush to exit. That same lady now stared at him with cold hatred from across the room—Evie Plummer.

Dain met Evie's cold, hard stare with one of his own. His mind began assessing the woman standing before him. Outwardly, she was still the beautiful woman he remembers seeing. She had a few more strands of gray in her otherwise dark hair. The lines marking her eyes and around her mouth gave mute testimony that she had lived more years than she would have probably admitted. Even with the loose trousers and baggie-fitting shirt it was apparent she carried a well-proportioned figure. Dain had a gut feeling that she was wound almost as tight as Colonel Bullard. An inner voice cautioned him to: "Walk ease, boy, she's about ready to pop her cork." The Colt .44 strapped to her right hip was further evidence that she wasn't to be dismissed lightly.

One question Dain's observation had failed to answer was: what possible connection could there be between the Evie in Hot Springs, Arkansas and the Evie standing before him here in this cabin? That, of course, brought another question to mind. Had Evie been acquainted with his mother? Or was the same woman he had seen in Hot Springs? It sure looked like her. Or was this all just purely coincidental? None of it made any sense.

Bullard interrupted Dain's thoughts. "Make no mistake about it, Bucklett, I will have that gold. You will convince Salas to cooperate or— well you can figure that out yourself. You convince him to give me the location of the war chest, and you have my solemn promise, as an officer and a gentlemen, no harm will come to either one of you. You see, neither of you have an option. It's just that simple. I hope I've made myself perfectly clear?"

"Quite clear, Colonel," Dain said firmly. "Now, I'll tell you something. I don't give a tinker's damn about your gold. I doubt very seriously if Pa has it or even knows anything about such a gold chest or otherwise. But that's neither here nor there," Dain paused, staring eye to eye with the colonel. "As of right now, you either feed us and keep us fed and well care for, or you may as well kill us both with no more messing around." Dain knew he was pushing his luck, but under the circumstances, what did he have to lose. Bullard wanted to know the whereabouts of the chest of gold, but how bad? If they couldn't escape, their chances were zero anyway. He and his father would have to be strong and in good physical shape when a break came their way.

Bullard laughed sarcastically, "Young man, I've got to hand it to you. You've got gall. But you're in no position to make demands."

Dain decided to make one more stab at trying to reason with Bullard. "You're making the mistake of your life, Colonel." Dain began; he turned his head to include Evie and Elkhart. "Don't you people realize that Pa would have turned any gold over to the Confederate government, if there was any such gold? If what you all say is true, he was acting under orders. You of all people know that, colonel, being a military man. Common sense will tell you he wasn't working alone. Besides, he . . ."

Elkhart interrupted. "That's what I've been telling you all along, Colonel," he glared. "That damn gold is long gone. Hell, it's probably in Washington by now."

"No!" Bullard shouted, furiously pacing back and forth, slapping his gloves against his thigh. "I know for a fact that it never turned up. I've got friends in the Capitol, and I've checked. Washington knows nothing about it. So, Bucklett has got to know where it's hidden, and I'm damn well going to find out where it is."

"Damn you, John," Evie snarled. "what he says makes sense." Her eyes narrowed to slits. "If you've brought me all this way to this god-forsaken country for nothing . . . ." her voice trailed off.

"What's the matter with you idiots?" Bullard squawked. "I'm telling you there's a fortune out there somewhere, and Bucklett knows where it is." Pausing, he turned to Dain, and said, "You've got until sunrise tomorrow. Now get in there and find out where that gold is or you're both dead men."

Elkhart lifted the crude plank that barred the door leading to the rear of the room, and shoved Dain roughly through the opening.

The room was in total darkness. Dain first thought they had lied to him, that he was alone. Gradually his eyes began to focus on what appeared to be a black void. Ever so slowly, he was able to make out various details in the darkened space. There was no warmth; it was extremely cold and damp, and it smelled like it had apparently been a root cellar of some sort. A space had been dug into the hillside before the one room soddy was erected to seal it from the outside. The small, wet enclosure was a death trap waiting to happen.

On hands and knees Dain crawled across the muddy floor until his hand touched the edge of a blanket. His father lay huddled, shivering from the cold, dank environment.

"Pa?" Dain's voice was barely above a whisper. "Pa. It's me, Dain. Pa? Pa?" He placed his hand on the old man's forehead. It was hot and clammy. Salas Bucklett was burning up with fever. Cold anger cut through Dain like a knife. He felt a fierce desire to strike out at those in the outer room.

Enraged, he pounded on the door. "Get some food and water in here. And hurry!" Dain shouted. "He's running a heavy, high fever. He's got to have some care."

"You get nothing until we find out where the gold is." Dain recognized Evie's voice. "Now, shut up and quit beating on the door."

"A dead man will tell you nothing," Dain countered harshly.

Someone mumbled something, and then an argument ensued before he heard the rattling of pots and pans. Minutes later, Elkhart called, "Back away from the door." Moments later, a bucket of water and a bowl of lukewarm stew were shoved through the open door.

Salas went into a fit of coughing as a small amount of water hit his throat.

"Who are you?" Salas asked faintly as Dain sponged his face.

"It's Dain, Pa."

"Aw, Son, you're here. So good . . ." he murmured weakly. "How did you find me?"

"Colonel Bullard brought me," Dain trying to sound positive. "Just take it easy, Pa. Everything is going to be just fine."

"I don't know, Son, I'm in a bad way." He took another sip of the cold liquid. "Where are your ma and Will?"

Dain felt torn, and was tempted for a moment to sugarcoat his answer. But he knew his father would never forgive him if he tried to beat around the bush or delay telling him about Ma. Compassion tugged sharply at his heart.

Salas was weak with fever and near starvation. But Dain didn't doubt for a moment his strong mental abilities.

"Ma's gone, Pa," Dain choked out the painful words. "She passed away very peacefully. Will and I, we buried her under that big oak tree in back of the house where she always liked to sit in the shade."

"Oh, no. Amy, my dear sweet Amy. May God rest her dear soul," Salas mourned. "Somehow, I had a feeling something was wrong."

A small shaft of light lay across the man's grief-stricken face. Dain watched as a single tear rolled down his father's weathered cheek.

Salas continued. "She was one hell of a good woman, Son. There's none better, God knows. I didn't do right by her when I up and left like I did, but she seemed to understand. She deserved better. I guess that's why the good Lord took her."

"That's no way to talk, Pa," Dain said soothingly. "Ma loved you a mighty lot, and what you did, you did for her. She knew that. She wouldn't want you to be fretting over her now. She'd want you to keep going ahead just like you've always done."

"Maybe you're right, Son. But still . . ." he sniffed, unashamed of the tears. "What about Will?"

"He and Booger Red are out there somewhere following our trail," Dain said, praying it was true. "I've not seem them, but I've got a feeling they're close by."

Dain looked around the small cramped enclosure. There was a small shaft of light coming from the outer room through a match-size knothole in an otherwise solid wooden door.

"I've got to figure a way to get us out of here," he whispered. "We can't afford to wait for Will. He'll likely be held up by the blizzard the same as we are. It might be a while before he can pick up our trail again, if at all. So we can't bank on that."

"Dain, you watch out for that Bullard," Salas cautioned, pushing aside the spoon of stew Dain held to his mouth. "He can't be trusted, neither can Evie. She is as wicked and vile as they come, the most vengeful person on God's green Earth."

"We'll talk later, Pa," Dain assured him. "Right now, I want you to eat some more. You've got to get over this fever, and get your strength back."

"Just a little more water," Salas said, feebly shaking his head. "I just want to rest."

As his father slept, Dain began to search, more by feel than by sight, for anything which could be useful for an escape—something, anything to give him hope.

Bullard said he had until sunrise. Dain had no idea how long he had now. But beyond the door, low voices continued as Dain's mind worked feverishly for an avenue of escape. Reluctantly, he gave up. Squatted near his father, he felt his forehead. He was sure the fever was a bit less. He said a quick, sincere prayer for continued improvement.

Raised voices from the next room brought Dain to the door. He was unable to distinguish words, but an argument was clearly in progress. The front door slammed. Listening a moment longer, he was sure only Evie and Elkhart remained.

After giving it some thought, Dain figured there was not even a slim chance that he could trick the two of them in an attempt to get away. It would be too big a chance with his father's life. Overpowering Evie and Elkhart was a little too risky, and not only that, the others could return to the cabin at any time.

It was imperative to get Salas to a safe place as soon as possible. Even if they were fortunate enough to escape, where could they go? His father was too weak to be of any assistance, even though he was familiar with these mountains. How was he going to care for him once they were free?

Dain worried that the fever and lack of food and medicine might not be his father's only problem. Dain noticed his father's flinching while he attempted to prop him in an upright position in order to give him food and water. It could be only some minor bruising, but at this point Dain couldn't be sure. He was afraid he might have some internal injury.

As he was thinking, Dain continued to walk slowly around the enclosure, running his hands along the packed dirt and rock walls. The texture of small roots and wood stems triggered a childhood memory.

As kids, he and Will often explored old home places and caves. During their exploration of one old homestead, Will had suddenly disappeared from his side. Will had fallen through a hole in the floor into a cellar-like pit below the house. Exploring further, they found he had plunged through a weakened area of an old dugout from an adjoining collapsed building.

The memory gave Dain new hope. Maybe, just maybe, he could find a weak spot overhead. Most of these old Soddy's were dug into the hillside and covered with pine boughs and twigs with a mixture of mud and grass.

Slowly and carefully, Dain began probing the ceiling. He felt across, back and across again, back and forth, many times. His arms were beginning to ache, and he was about to give up the cause, when suddenly, his fingertips brushed the smallest of protrusions, a tiny twig of a root. It was much too short to grasp with his fingers. Dain grabbed his father's soup spoon.

He felt like shouting as he dug into the earth, using fingers of one hand to pull on the twig, as he gouged with the other. He stopped occasionally to tug the twig which steadily grew longer to his touch. Eventually, he was rewarded with a bettor hold. He tugged firmly; it gave way, and down came a handful of dirt.

The small amount of earth hitting the floor sounded like a clap of thunder to Dain's ears. He waited expectantly, waiting for the door to fly open at any moment. He placed his ear to the door. The noise emitting from the other room sounded more like two animals moaning, grunting, with an occasional deep-throated growl. Dain was no prude, but he was shocked.

They weren't . . . he thought. They couldn't be . . . . Diddy-dad-burn if they weren't. Hell, the whole roof could be caving in, and they wouldn't hear a thing. He turned and began digging in earnest.

NINE

Evie stood before the fire with her back to Elkhart. Quickly, she smoothed her hair in order, and then dealt with her clothing, brushing and tugging things into shape. Her thoughts raced as she berated herself for taking such a stupid risk. Yet, she was determined, at the first opportunity, to draw that fool Elkhart into her plans. If it took her body to entice him, so be it. She was determined to control the use of the gold once it was found. She had made the same offer to Salas. Stupid, stupid man, she thought him and his pathetic honor. Well, he could die with his honor. The desire she'd once felt for him had long turned into hatred. There was one thing she sought almost as much as she wanted the gold; she wanted to be the one to pull the trigger on Salas as he was taking his last breath. She wanted to laugh in his face and tell him she was the one responsible for Amy's death. Yes, that would satisfy her thirst for revenge. Then, she would leave the god-forsaken country.

As Evie fantasized, Elkhart was busy with his own plans. He almost laughed aloud as he watched Evie. She really thought he couldn't see what she was attempting to accomplish. Sure he would take what she had to offer. After all, she had a great body and knew how to use it. He would even kill Bullard or any of the others for her, and be glad to. But when the gold was found, he didn't expect her to be around to help him spend it. She definitely did not fit into his plans whatsoever.

*   *   *

Dain worked feverishly, praying that any noise he made wouldn't be heard. Once the moaning sounds subsided, he worked more cautiously. The going was painstaking slow. He filled his hat and then spread it carefully on the floor so that it wouldn't be so conspicuously noticed if he had an unexpected visitor.

Using his fingertips to dig at the dirt, they became raw and began to bleed. The small, sharp stones and dirt had long since grated away the outer skin. His nails were the first to disappear, but he work on.

Dain sensed it was well after midnight. The temperature had dropped drastically. Dain's physical exertion had brought some warmth to his body, but he knew the same was not true with his father. Dain thought gravely about exposing his father to the hazardous elements once they had, hopefully, escaped. But staying in their present situation was almost certain death. He could only hope his father would have some idea of a safe destination once they were free.

Dain returned to his father's side. He knelt and placed his hand gently on his father's shoulder. "Pa?" he whispered. "Pa, I think I've found a way out of here. I'm digging a hole in the ceiling. We can—"

"No Son. I'll never be able to make it," he answered urgently. "You go, Son. Save yourself."

"No way, Pa," Resolve was firm in his whisper. "We go together. Besides, I don't know this country; you do. You're going to have to show me the way. Is there a town or settlement nearby where we can go for help?"

"There's a trappers' hangout, but you'll get no help from any of them," Salas answered haltingly, his voice hardly above a whisper. "They'd turn you over to Bullard for the price of a shot of rotgut whiskey."

Dain saw his father was becoming agitated. He held a cup of water to his lips, and after he drank a little, Dain said, "Get a little rest now, Pa. We'll talk later."

Dain, concentrating on his digging, had long since lost track of time. Occasionally, he stopped and listened at the door, but thank goodness, all was quiet. He was getting slightly discouraged when suddenly cold air hit him in the face. He inhaled sharply and began frantically tearing at the small opening with bloody hands. The beautiful sight of a clear, starry night brought a burst of renewed energy. Bit by bit the small opening became a nice large hole.

When a sound hit Dain's ears, his hands stilled immediately; a bed squeaked. Was someone approaching the door? They had only to open the door and it would all be over. Quickly, he lay down near the door, and pretended a rhythmic snore. His gut told him someone had their ear to the door. Minutes passed. Dain didn't relax until he heard the bed squeak again. The squeak had the sound of someone lying down again. He waited several minutes before he dropped his snore to a more light breathing before stopping altogether. Only when he heard the sound of snoring from the other side of the door, did he resume his efforts. The opening was now large enough for his wide shoulders; he felt it was now or never.

He now had another obstacle to overcome. How could he get his father through the hole without making too much noise?

"Pa? Pa, wake up." Dain's whispers sounded like a loud drumbeat to his own ears.

"Pa? Pa?" Dain whispered again only a little louder.

"Huh?" Salas answered weakly.

"Come on, Pa; we're getting out of here. Don't make a sound," Dain warned. "No matter what happens, don't make a sound. Our lives depend on it."

"You go, Son. Leave me be," his voice barely audible.

"No, Pa. Remember, we go together," Dain's mouth was against his father's ear.

Knowing he could wait no longer, he helped his father to his feet. He soon had the blanket tied securely around Salas's shoulders. The threadbare blanket would provide slight protection from the elements, but it was all they had, and being tied securely would provide something for Dain to grasp when getting his father through the hole in the ceiling.

Dain was shocked at the amount of weight Salas had lost. Only the sure knowledge that they were on the brink of their last chance gave Dain the strength to boost Salas upward through the hole. Salas was able to help somewhat by pulling up with his elbows once his torso cleared the opening. As soon as his feet were clear, Dain jumped straight up, got a handhold and pulled himself until he was clearly and completely through the hole.

They did it! Dain was elated they had gotten this far. Dain raised his face to the sky and mouthed a silent, "Thank You."

Dain could see no sign of horses anywhere. They were probably in some meadow close by, but they had no time to look for them. By the stars and the slight glow in the eastern horizon, Dain knew they had very little time to get away.

He picked up his father as a man would carry a small child, and started for the tree line up the slope behind the dugout.

The dark gray of a new day cut the serrated outline of the peaks in the east before Dain unburdened himself. To make better time, he kept to the contours of the land, neither going uphill nor down, except to bypass obstacles. As desperate as his was to put distance between him and the cabin, he still took care to cover their tracks.

"Where are we, Son?" Salas asked, his teeth chattered feverishly.

"Don't rightly know, Pa," Dain answered. "After I left the dugout, I headed south and then I was forced to vary off to the west a little, when I ran into some heavy timber. Then I doubled back to the north, figuring to throw them off if they came across any of our tracks. But frankly, I haven't the foggiest idea where we're at or where I'm going."

"That running water I hear?" Salas asked softly.

"Yeah, Pa. There's a small trickle of a stream yonder. I figured this is as good a place as any to stop for awhile."

"Describe it to me."

"All I can see are a couple of beaver ponds and a small waterfall about five, say, maybe six feet high. There's lots of good size boulders and a trickle of water over the rocks."

"How far you guess-to-mate we are from the cabin?"

"Say— maybe as the crow flies. Oh—about two and a half miles, more or less, I reckon."

"This would be Malo Vaga Creek," Salas said haltingly through chattering teeth. "If'n it is . . . there's an old Indian trail, just north of here . . . . over a hog . . . . back ridge. There is a cache . . . in a . . . .

cave . . . . in some rocks . . . high up . . . on a bluff," He was shaking so badly he could barely get a word out.

"How far, Pa?"

No answer. Salas only mumbled and muttered in a low voice.

So Pa knew of a cache up in those hills someplace, Dain presumed. Apparently, there was a cave among some boulders, which was on the side of a bluff; which was north of their present position. But there was a hogback ridge they must go over first. That is, if this is the place Salas was thinking they were, as Dain described it. If it wasn't, then, they could be in trouble. But first he must find the old Indian trail Salas spoke of. It was a long shot, but it was the best Dain had to go on. They couldn't just sit here, that's for sure. They either had to move somewhere or they would be caught in the open. What's more, Salas needed decent shelter and medical care— and soon.

Their escape would be discovered shortly, if it hasn't been already. From now on he would have to walk like a ghost on water, be more cautious than ever at concealing their tracks.

Dain gave his father some water from the nearby stream. Then with feeble assistance from Salas, Dain was able to transfer his father to his back, making traveling somewhat easier.

Heading east, he crosses the small stream, keeping his eyes peeled for what could be construed as an Indian trail. After going a little ways Dain turned south keeping to the contours of the mountain. Coming into a clearing he found himself slipping and sliding on some shale. It's just what the doctor ordered, considering he could get across the rocky shale and sandstone without getting them both killed. It appeared the rocky shelf of shale and sandstone extended, and held, all the way to the bottom of the canyon some hundreds of feet below. It would be treacherous at best. Meticulously, Dain began picking his way down and across the precarious slope with his burden. Caution was utmost on his mind. One slip on dew-covered stone and they would find themselves tumbling over hundreds of feet to their death. There was nothing to arrest their plunge—no trees, no stumps, or rock outcroppings, just loose shale all the way down.

Twice, Dain thought their time had come. The last time had been far worse. The stone he chose for his next step appeared nice and flat and approximately twelve inches in diameter. From above it looked to be well supported, but no sooner had he put his foot on the stone, than two things happened; his father shifted his weight on his back, and the material underneath the stone crumbled to dust. The stone rolled all the way to the bottom, as Dain righted himself, and splashed into the creek below. The sound of a minor landslide echoed far down the canyon.

When they reached the bottom of the canyon, Dain stepped into the crystal clear, icy water, and turned north, upstream. He soon passed the point where he first entered the stream only a short while back. With any luck at all, the colonel and his people would be looking for him down south.

Hours later, Dain estimated they had covered a little over five miles, a rough five miles, much of it being uphill. He had yet to come across anything which could be called an Indian trail. His feet were numb from wading in the ice cold water, and he was exhausted from crawling over more beaver dams than he cared to count. He kept to the creek relentlessly, but the stream was beginning to peter out, now only a slight trickle now and then. He would have to leave it soon.

Dain stopped occasionally to listen for any pursuit, but heard nothing but the wind singing in the tall pines. Finding a rocky ledge that hung out over the stream, Dain laid his father down on a warm slab. He faced his father, and with cupped hands coaxed a small amount of the cool water down his parched throat.

Dain began to wonder, had Pa known what he was saying when he spoke of a cache and a cave, or was he hallucinating from the fever? If it was the fever talking, they were in bad trouble.

Dain, wet, cold and exhausted, laid back on the warm rock next to his father. The warm energy of the sun was a welcome to his fatigued body. He closed his eyes, trying to remember how long it had been since he slept.

Suddenly, his eyes opened; he had not intended to doze off, but he must have. But what awakened him? He saw three mule tail deer drinking downstream. Startled at the turn of his head, they darted back into the safety of the timber.

Dain left his father and followed what appeared to be an animal trail. Just maybe it would be the one he was looking for. Indians, as well as white men, often followed the trails used by animals. Being creatures of habit animals choose the easiest and most sensible route through the forest to their watering holes. They knew these routes to be relatively safe from danger.

Returning to the rock he found his father awake. "I found a trail, Pa. I don't know if it's the one you spoke of."

"We get to the top of that ridge, I should be able to direct you, Son," he shivered. "You should have left me back there."

"I'll not have you talking like that, Pa," Dain declared. "We'll make it."

Salas looked at his son with drooping eyelids. "Son, if I don't make it, you get to Maestas."

"What's Maestas got to do with all this?"

"He's an old friend. Trust him," Salas said, sighing heavily. "He'll have something for you and Will."

"Are you talking about the gold shipment?" Dain didn't believe that was the case.

Salas smiled wearily, and said, "Better than gold, son." His voice was only a whisper as he drifted off again.

Dain was unsure if he drifted off to sleep or unconsciousness. Carefully he lifted his father once again to his back. He kept off the trail, but traveled parallel to it so as not to leave any sign of their passing. He was extremely watchful with each step he took. He had lived in the mountains all his life and was trail-wise of man and beast. He took great heed to use the underbrush to hide his tracks and eased through them so as not to break or disturb the limbs.

He was nearing the crest of the mountain when he noticed the hogback ridge his father must have been talking about. It lay to the northwest of his present position, but in the general direction of the trail he was following.

Keeping the old trail in sight, he went another mile when he saw the rocky outcropping he hoped was their destination. It took him over an hour to find the mouth of the cave. He had bypassed it on the way up, by only a few feet. The light was fading fast as he pushed aside some brush oak growing between two leaning slabs of limestone forming an inverted V which covered the opening to the cave.

At first it appeared to be a mountain lion's den, but once he crawled inside, Dain was amazed at the size of the large interior.

There was a fairly good supply of hides, blankets, and food. Dain was relieved to see a pile of dried wood that would emit little, if any, tell-tale smoke. There was also an old, but useable, Henry .44, a Colt Peacemakers .45, with ammunition for both, and even a Barlow pocket knife. Dain learned later that the cache was shared be a number of trappers and frontiersmen who use the cave in times of need. In a very short time Salas was resting comfortably under a pile of pelts, wrapped in worn, but very welcomed blankets. Once Dain a fire going, he rinsed out a battered old skillet, and filled it with snow water to make some much needed coffee.

From the cache of supplies, which were packed in buried tin, he found jerky, some salt-cured bacon, coffee and even some salt and sugar. He could hardly believe his luck. There were a few tins of tomatoes and a bladder-sack of dried beans. Everything was packed so varmints couldn't get to it.

With the water boiling, Dain shaved in some jerky and added a can of tomatoes for some stew, keeping the can to use as a coffee mug. The Barlow was fairly rusty, but he made good use of it be by fashioning a spoon from a piece of wood.

After persuading his father to take some broth, he ate what remained of the cowboy stew. With the coffee on the fire, he crawled out of the mouth of the cave to check their hide-a-way. The sun had long since set and the temperature had dropped drastically; the sky had become overcast with low, storm-threatening clouds. Looking around, he was satisfied no tell-tale smoke or light would give away their position. He returned to find Salas still feverish, but sleeping peacefully.

As Dain sat nursing his coffee from the tomato can, he became aware of how tired he was—completely exhausted. Every bone and muscle in his bode ached.

Dain stared into the fire. He was surprised that the leaping, dancing, ever-changing flames brought him a deep measure of peace. Peace brought with it a sure belief that the future would deal kindly with his family. It seemed so right to include Trin in the family circle.

Dain's thoughts touched briefly on the strange, distinctive pull of the campfire—its comfort that drew a man to seek the indiscriminately offered solace.

Dain was brought back to his present circumstances when he heard his father murmur, "Amy, Amy."

Dain remembered a time, long past. He was very young at the time, and quite ill with fever of some sort. He spent the night wedged between his parents. It must have been close to morning when the combined body heat from his parents had finally broken his fever and allowed peaceful rest. He recalled his mother's joy when he declared himself hungry enough to eat the following morning.

Dain, with moist eyes, stripped off his outer clothing, crawled under the blankets and wrapped his arms around his father beneath the heavy covering of pelts and blankets.

TEN

Will Bucklett attempted to burrow deeper into the snow bank. Somewhere, off in the distance, he could hear muttering voices. He was aware Indians always returned for their dead. If they found him, he would surely lose his hair. He attempted to move his body forward for better concealment, but for some unknown reason his limbs refused to cooperate.

He had no idea how much time had passed since the Indians left the clearing. The slightest movement of his left arm brought a sharp, nauseating pain. But as the pain subsided, he became aware he was no longer lying in the snow. He recognized a very invigorating fragrance of cooking food, and another scent, quite different, yet pleasantly satisfying. Lilacs! Yes, that was it, lilacs! His eyelids seemed unusually heavy as he tried to force them open. Finally, the weights lifted, and he begins trying to focus on his surroundings.

He was in a four poster bed between brilliant white sheets. The adobe walls surrounding him were covered with colorful tapestries. In a small niche between two oak-framed figurines stood a Madonna hold the Christ Child. Will was at a complete loss. Why was he in a church lying in a four poster bed that smelled like lilacs?

Suddenly, he realized he is not alone. He turned his head and saw a dark-haired angel smiling down at him. It took him a moment to remember where he had seen the angel. It was the lady from Ludlow, the one who gave him her horse, Juanita. Her large, dark eyes were well spaced; her olive skin was smooth and clear, like an unblemished sunset. Her hair hung loose over her shoulders; and a white Spanish lace shawl covered her head. Her face was one of intelligences and humor with just a hint of sorrow. Will wondered at the expression of sadness, and wished he could somehow replace it with joy.

"How do you feel, Senor?" Her voice was as soft as the morning breeze.

His lips moved, but nothing came out. On the second try, he croaked, "I could use a drink of water." His throat felt as if he had swallowed a bucket of rusty nails and washed them down with pine knots.

Juanita held a glass of water to his lips, he heard a door open. Will wasn't ready for the intrusion. Juanita's company was sufficient for all his wants and needs.

"How are you feeling, Will?" Trin asked, her face beaming. An older man stood behind her.

"I'll be okay unless I die due to all this kindness and attention I'm getting," Will grumbled.

"Don't be an old grouch," she ordered, her mood unaltered.

The man standing behind Trin was tall and slim. His dark hair was touched with silver along the temples. The well-trimmed mustache gave him the appearance of a man of means.

"Welcome to my hacienda, Senor Will Bucklett. I am Antonio Maestas, and I understand you have already met my daughter."

"It is an honor to meet you, sir," Will responded, not liking the idea of meeting Juanita's father while lying flat on his back. "How long have I been here?"

"Two days," Don Maestas informed him. "Pico, whom you have met, and Miguel were driving some cattle down from the high country when they heard shooting. They tell me you make an excellent account of yourself."

"Father, he must eat now and have his rest," Juanita reminded him. "You can have your conversation later when he is much stronger."

"Got no time to be lying around," Will said. "My family is in danger, and they'll need my help."

"You will not be so foolish as to leave your bed in such a weak condition, Senor Bucklett," Juanita said firmly. "Besides, your clothing is now being mended."

For the first time, Will realized he was buck naked under the smooth, white sheets. He was unable to avoid the flush of redness as it covered his face. He could only hope no one noticed or would have the decency not to mention it.

Will welcomed the distraction as Don Maestas said, "She is correct, Senor Will. You must rest and regain your strength. I have men throughout the area looking for my friend Salas. As soon as one of my men locates him, you will be the first to know, I can assure you." He turned and walked toward the door. Before leaving he turned and said, "If you have a need, please do not hesitate to inform me. You are most welcome here. My hacienda is your hacienda, Senor."

As he left, a slightly plump maid entered, carrying a large tray of steaming food. She grinned knowingly at Juanita as she set the tray on the bedside table. Before leaving, she came close to Juanita and whispered rather loudly, "Si, hombre magnifico."

Juanita's face turned crimson as she spoke sharply to the maid, who left the room laughing.

"What about Booger Red?" Will asked.

"Juan says he will not be able to ride for a few more days, but he is coming along nicely," Trin answered. With a grin, she continued, "I believe he rather likes all the attention he has been getting, especially from the maid, Maria. Still, he says he is anxious to be up and about."

After Trin left, Juanita insisted on helping Will with his food. Each time their eyes met, they both looked away quickly, Juanita with uncharacteristic shyness and Will wondering just who had helped him to the present state of undress, yet not daring to ask.

After Will had taken all the food he could hold, Juanita left with the tray. She returned shortly and offered him a cup. "You have lost much blood, Senor Bucklett. You must drink this."

"Will."

She looked at him puzzled.

"My name is Will."

"Si." The smallest of smiles touched her satin lips.

He took a swallow from the cup. Gagging, he asked, "What is this stuff?"

She smiled widely, a near laugh. "It is a drink made with herbs found only in Mexico. It will help return the blood you have lost to your body. Please, drink?"

Will, enjoying her pleasant smile, thought, if it doesn't kill me first. It brought to mind all the doses of castor oil his mother forced him to swallow.

"I'm very sorry about your horse," he said apologetically. "He was a fine animal, just as you said."

"Oh, do not worry, Senor Will," The way she emphasized his name was pleasing to Will's ears. "He found his way home not long after Pico and Miguel brought you here."

"I'm pleased," his eyelids were beginning to droop. "I'd sure hate for any harm to come to that horse." His began to slur his words. "I'm feeling mighty sleepy all of a sudden. What was in that drink anyway?"

Juanita's laugh was softly mischievous as Will's last words were hardly audible.

As he sank into a deep sleep, Juanita started to pull the covers up around his shoulders. She glanced quickly toward the door to make sure she was alone; she eased back the covers, baring his chest. His right shoulder was bandaged heavily due to the arrow wound. There was no fresh bleeding. The gunshot wound he received in Ludlow was healing nicely and was no longer bandaged. Slowly, gently, she replaced the sheets.

Will had always been an early riser and the following morning was no exception. He awoke peacefully refreshed and amazingly alert, his mind clear and undisturbed. Swinging his feet to the floor he experienced some light-headedness, but it quickly passed.

Surprisingly, he felt little pain in his right shoulder, and only a slight itchy sensation from the gunshot wound in his left arm.

A pleasant aroma of cooking food reminded Will of his hunger. His clothes, washed and mended, were folded neatly on a nearby chair. He dressed with little trouble, being careful with his most recent wound.

At the foot of a wide staircase, Will followed the sound of cheerful voices beyond a broad archway.

Pico, his hat hanging by the chin strap around his neck, was the first to see him. "Aw, Senor, it is good that you come back to the living," he said holding out his hand. His grasp was firm yet mindful of the wounded right arm. His expression was friendly; the happy-go-lucky demeanor, very much a part of this man, did not conceal his excellent abilities.

Juanita's back had been to Will as he entered the room. She whirled around. "Senor, you should not be . . . you are not ready yet . . . ." She stopped, embarrassed at her outburst. She turned away quickly.

"You will join us, Senor?" Don Maestas interjected, preventing his daughter from further discomfort.

"Thank you," Will responded graciously. "But if I may, I would like to see Booger Red first."

"Of course, I understand," Don Maestas replied. "As he is occupied with his breakfast in his room at this time, perhaps you will allow me to accompany you to him when you have attended to your own needs?"

Will nodded his agreement as he took a seat next to Pico. Turning to Pico, he said, "Seems like I owe you and your friend my life, amigo. I'm mighty obliged."

Pico waved away the gratitude, "De nada, de nada, Senor."

"Call me Will."

"Si, Senor Will," Pico's grin widened, accepting the offer of immediate friendship.

"How are your wounds this morning?" Don Maestas asked.

"Little stiff yet, but well enough for riding, I reckon."

Juanita regained her composure. "But you should have more strength. You could possibly open your wound if you travel too quickly."

"I appreciate your concern, but I'll be moving out as soon as possible." He turned toward the don. "That is, of course, if I could barter with you for some food and the use of a horse."

Juanita, hands on hip, started to speak. She was forestalled when her father held his hand up to indicate silence. He spoke in Spanish for a moment, and turned back to Will. "Excuse me, Senor Bucklett, I do not intend to be rude, but I was telling my daughter men's business is not to be confused with the thoughts of women."

After breakfast, Don Maestas lit a long slender cigar after offering one to Will and Pico. They talked companionably as they walked toward Booger Red's room.

Will was unprepared for the emotions he felt when he saw Booger Red; the man was much like a second father. Each looked deeply into the eyes of the other for a moment, each profoundly grateful the other was well on the way to recovery.

Booger Red stood stiffly, ramrod straight in concession to his tightly wrapped ribs. His right hand was heavily swathed in splints and bandages. Dark bruises were throughout his physical resilient frame.

"Glad to see those skunks caused no lasting harm," Will said clasping Red's shoulders.

"Humph," Red said with a snort. "Skunk much stink, no bite."

His remarks were met with laughter and agreement by those in the room.

"Come," Don Maestas invited. "We will have coffee and discuss the plans to be made."

The dining table now cleared, the four men soon became enveloped in a cloud of cigar smoke. The Don began, "Pico, you will prepare the men for a long ride and see that they are well armed."

"Si, patron."

"You've heard something from your men?" Will asked hopefully.

"No, Senor," the don answered. "I'm afraid not."

"That being the case, I think it would be better if I went alone. One man can travel faster and I'd be a lot less noticeable than a group of riders."

"But, Senor Will," Pico objected, "these men are killers. They will not hesitate to shoot you down like chicken in barrel."

"I go, too," Red said resolutely.

"I appreciate it, Booger Red, but, no," Will said firmly. "I'd like it if you stay, and when the Don's men find some news, get it to me."

"How will you do this?" Pico asked.

"Booger Red knows how to find me. This is the fastest and safest way," Will answered. He turned to Don Maestas, "I'd be obliged for the loan of a good horse."

The don considered for a moment. "It will be as you say, Will. It is an honor to be of service to my friend's son." He turned and issued the necessary orders to Pico. "He will have the appaloosa; also see that he has the weapons he requires. I will prepare another more detailed map which could be most useful to him."

"Si, Don Maestas. It will be done as you say." He smiled as he took his leave.

Don Maestas resumed his seat at the head of the large table. "I would appreciate your indulgence for a short time. I feel that it is important you be made aware of some things which have occurred in the past." He paused, glancing between his two visitors. "I will not hinder with the search for Salas and your brother Dain at this time. I will wait for a little while, let's say three days. If you have not returned in three days, or I have not had word from you, I will take action of my own."

He held up his hand as Will started to speak. "One moment, please, Senor," he paused. "I first met Salas many years ago in Chihuahua, Mexico. We soon found we could trust and care for each other as brothers. The reason will be made clear to you at the proper time.

"It was very bad times in Mexico. There was much talk of war. The Texans desired to become part of the United States. El Presidente Lopez de Santa Anna forced many young men into his army. Those of us who did not wish to fight for the el president fled to the Sierra de la Madera Mountains. There was little to do to occupy our time, so at the suggestion of your padre, we began to search for gold. Neither of us really expected to succeed in such a search, you understand. But for some unknown reason, Dios touched our hands.

"We found enough gold to insure great wealth. However, with all the wealth we found, there were still problems we had to overcome. Our food supply was dangerously low. To leave the mountains meant we would surely be arrested. There, of course, came the point where the risk must be taken. I went to Sahuaripa, a small village, to obtain needed supplies. There I was arrested but was able to escape.

"When I returned to the mountains, Salas and I decided it would be wise to hide our gold and return after the war was at an end. From there Salas and I went to Santa Fe. We were again found and arrested by the soldiers of the el president. We were to be shot. As we were attempting to escape, we were separated because Salas tried to draw the soldiers away from me. But my horse was killed and I was thrown to the ground. I hit my head on a stone in my fall from the horse. I was unconscious for a long time. Both Salas and the soldiers thought I was dead. Later, after talking to some men who observed this, I was told the soldiers surrounded Salas on a high cliff. When I searched this place, I found much blood. I think my friend is also dead. I do not think he would not survive a fall from such a high place. But, I do not think the soldiers returned with his body. It is not until many years had passed that I learned, with great joy, that my dear friend Salas, is indeed alive." Don Maestas paused. "Come; allow me to show you a map."

Will and Booger Red followed Don Maestas into another room. On the wall, behind a massive heavy Spanish desk, he pointed to a very large map. "With the gold from the Sierra de la Madre Mountains, I acquired much land and wealth. One-half of all that I have belongs to Salas."

Speechless, Will stared transfixed at the area of the map Don Maestas circled with his finger. Will looked at Red in astonishment. Booger Red only shrugged.

"After I was able to retrieve the gold, I came to Colorado as a stranger." The don explained further, "Here I have made a home for myself as well as for Salas. He will remain a brother to me, always."

Will exhaled. "Does he know about this?"

"Of course," Don Maestas answered. "I was in Denver shortly before the end of your civil war. I met a man there and he spoke of a Major Salas Bucklett who served in the army of the south. When he told me the major's home was in Arkansas. I was overjoyed, yet afraid to believe it to be my friend from Mexico. I sent a message to him.

When he arrived here some time after the war, I surprised him with all of this. It was truly a joyous occasion. He was most anxious to bring his family here."

"Must be a thousand acres there," Will estimated.

"A little over two hundred and forty-thousand," the don answered with pride. "More than sixty thousand head of cattle and more than two thousand head of some of the finest Spanish saddle stock if all of Colorado. Half of which belongs to the Bucklett family."

"If Pa thought you were dead, why didn't he go back after the gold?" Will inquired.

"I was the one who actually hid it. There was much trust between us. Even though there was much danger in those days from the militia, we thought, as young men do, that we could conquer all the obstacles, even death. We planned to hide the treasure this one certain evening. We set upon our mission when we encountered an old mountain man. He had the misfortune to have broken his leg in a fall." Don Maestas paused, remembering back. "I shall never forget the name of the old man; it was most strange, as he was. His name was Pincher, a very unique individual."

A smile touched his lips. With a shake of his head, he brought himself back to the subject.

"Salas suggested, rather than postponing our plan that I would proceed to hide our wealth in a secure place. I very much regret now that we failed to discuss, the exact location of the cache."

Although he believed the don's story, Will found it difficult to readily absorb. Yet, he knew this had to be the treasure which his father had spoken of in his letter.

Will was eager to begin his search and lost no time in starting his preparations. He expressed to Don Maestas his appreciation for his hospitality and to Juanita for her excellent care.

A short time later, he was ready to travel. He checked his cinch and was stepping into the stirrup when Juanita came up to stand at the railing. Her eyes were moist as she looked up at Will.

"Go with God," she said softly.

ELEVEN

Evie was not in the best of moods when she climbed from between the course, threadbare blankets. It was so bitterly cold in the shabby cabin, if you could call it a cabin. It was more like a hole in the ground as far as she was concerned. Elizabeth Collstern Plummer, the daughter of a once successful Kentucky plantation owner, was stuck in a mud dugout in the middle of only God knew where.

She had to admit to herself she enjoyed last night's little escapade with Elkhart. Not from the physical enjoyment, but she felt now that Elkhart would fit into her scheme much better than she had at first anticipated. It served John Bullard right, she thought. The very idea, of John flying off the handle like he had and then go riding off into the night leaving her with that clumsy lout. He probably spent the night messing with that stupid little whore she'd seen him talking to in Wildwood.

Would Elkhart stand with her until the finish? How far could he be trusted? Not far enough, you could bet on that. She knew she would have to stay one step ahead of him, or he would toss her aside like a worn-out shoe.

After he left last night to sleep in the shelter the men had rigged up down near the meadow, she mentally kicked herself. He had given her no information, while she, on the other hand, had blurted out everything on her mind. But still there was no doubt that he would be willing, and quite capable eliminating anyone who may get in their way. That's all she really wanted from him anyway. Still, she wished she hadn't told him about Amy Bucklett. But she could see no way he could use that information to his advantage; yet, she would have to be more cautious in the future. He was not the first man she had used to her benefit and probably would not be the last. She took pride in her ability in handling men and money.

Cheered by the thought of being a grand lady once again, she stoked the coals in the stone fireplace and added kindling until the flames caught. By the light of the fire she notice Tobe's bedding was still rolled against to wall.

Now what in the hell could have happened to him, she wondered. That was another thorn in her side she was concerned about. She'd had about all she could take from her nit-wit brother. He was always hanging onto her coattail like some snot-nosed kid—just like Papa, she thought; a milk-sopping, lily-livered brat, not worth the powder to blow him to hell. But still he was her blood brother. Secretly she hoped he would get lost and that worthless, manure-stinking cowboy, Skeets, along with him.

It was still dark outside; she had no idea what time it was. She just knew she couldn't sleep with all those infernal rats scratching and running up the walls. The irritating sounds kept her awake most of the night. At one point she thought Dain and Salas had been up to something, maybe trying to escape, but after listening at the door until she thought she would freeze to death, she decided it had to be the rats. Tobe had played with those beastly rodents he found around the barn when they were kids, often teasing her with them. God, how she hate him! But that stopped after she planted a pitchfork in his butt. Elizabeth Collstern Plummer knew how to handle men, one way or another.

Evie sat huddled near the fireplace with a blanket around her shoulders, "Where is everybody?" She muttered aloud.

As if in answer to her question, Tobe barged in the door. "Hi, Sis," he said sheepishly. "Where is everyone? Dang, it's cold out there. I think it's going to snow again."

"Where in the hell have you been, you stupid imbecile?" Evie flared. "I swear, Tobe, if you mess this deal up for me, I'll kill you. You hear me?"

"Yeah, sure Sis," he said hanging his head. "But we should have stayed back in Kentucky. Why'd we have to come all the way out here? There's nothing here but mountains and ticks."

"Damn, Tobe." If she didn't hate her fool brother so much, she might feel halfway sorry for him. "I've told you a hundred times. Can't you remember anything? Are you always going to be so simple-minded?"

"I'm not simple-minded and you know it," he said defensively. "What you all are doing to that old man in there is sinful, and you know it. It just ain't right! If you weren't my sister, I'd turn you all over to the law."

"You'll keep that sort of thought to yourself, you hear." Evie threatened. "If I ever—"

Before she could finish, Colonel Bullard walked in followed by Elkhart and Skeets.

Bullard glared at Evie and then at Tobe. "You keep that damn brother of yours in line or there'll be one less to split with. You get that? I told you he'd get lost. He's lucky Skeets found him."

"Yeah, all that night ridin' put a mighty powerful hunger on a man," Skeets said.

"That can wait," Bullard insisted. "Elkhart, get those two out here. I'm finished waiting."

Elkhart opened the door, put his head inside, and yelled, "They're gone!"

All eyes looked at Elkhart, disbelief on their faces.

"What?" Evie was the first to respond.

"They've vamoosed, escaped. They ain't there. You know, like gone," he repeated. "How else can I say it? There's a hole in the roof big enough to ride a horse through."

"You're lying!" the colonel blurted out angrily, as he jumped up. He knocked over his chair and rushed to the door to see for himself. Seeing the opening Dain had been able to dig out during the night, his control vanished. In his fury, he turned sharply and struck out at the nearest thing to him. That happened to be one person—Elkhart.

"Why you bunch of sorry, no good . . . ." The back of his hand caught Elkhart across the mouth. Elkhart rocked back on his heels, momentarily stunned by the unexpected blow. Taking a couple of steps backward, his revolver suddenly flashed in his fist. The roar of the blazing six-gun was deafening in the enclosed quarters. When the smoke finally cleared, Colonel John Bullard's body pumped crimson blood into the Colorado dirt floor.

Tobe and Evie stood paralyzed, eyes widened as they watched the body twitched momentarily before it became motionless. Skeets stood aside with his gun in his fist, his eyes on Elkhart. Their eyes locked death only an instant away. "You have any objections?" Elkhart asked, a sinister smile touching his lips.

Skeets slowly shook his head, holstering his pistol. "No objections. He asked for it. I guess he had it coming. Anyway, I'm lightin' a shuck. I never did cotton to the way the wind blows around here."

"Not before we find the Bucketts, you won't," Elkhart said mildly. "After that I don't give a damn what you do or where you go." He looked toward Evie and Tobe. "What about you two?"

Tobe, green around the gills, looked as if he was about to empty his stomach. Elkhart knew Tobe was nothing but a wet fish and gave him no more thought than a bothersome fly. He had a fleeting thought: just get rid of him here and now; but how would Evie respond to him killing her brother? He doubted if she cared one way or another. After last night, he felt he knew which side of the fence she would jump. But he had learned that when it came to women, a man would be better off trying to guess which direction a bird would fly.

"All right, I'll tell you all how it's going to be," Elkhart stared hard at Evie. "From here on out you all dance to the tune I play or you don't dance at all. Understood?"

"How could you be so damn stupid?" Evie yelled. "Now we'll never find out about the gold or even if there is any. You've blundered away my only chance to—"

"Like hell," Elkhart interrupted. "If anyone knows how to get the Buckletts to talk, it's me. Don't you worry any about that? Once we find 'em, they'll be glad to tell me anything I want to know. You can bet on it."

"You'd better, mister," Evie warned him. "John and I had this all worked out, and if you fiddle around and mess things up, you'll live to regret it."

"No!" Tobe squeaked. "Sis, this ain't right. Let's get out of here and—"

"Shut up, Tobe," Evie said angrily. "All John ever wanted to do was give orders. What did he ever do for you, except run you down and make you look foolish? John just wanted to play the big shot and where did that get him. Just keep your mouth shut, do what you're told, and everything will be all right."

Slowly, Tobe lowered himself into a chair. She was right, he had to admit. John always lorded it over him. He had been the most arrogant and domineering person he had ever known, except for his mother. So why make a fuss over someone he cared so little about anyway. At least John wouldn't be around to put crazy ideas into Evie's head anymore. Then there was the gold; with the gold, Evie and he could go back home and rebuild the plantation. That's really what he wanted, wasn't it? It took money to run a plantation, lots of money.

"All right," Elkhart said. "Let's go; they can't have gotten too far."

Two hours later they lost Dain's trail where he had entered the stream.

"They've got to be around here somewhere," Elkhart observed. "Spread out, and if anybody sees anything, fire a shot."

"They didn't just disappear into thin air," Evie said later when she met Elkhart in a small clearing some time later.

"Have you seen Tobe or Skeets?" Elkhart asked.

"No," Evie said, chuckling. "Tobe probably got lost again."

"What we need is a good tracker," Elkhart noted. "Let's get back to the cabin. I'll pack a few supplies and see if I can pick up their trail, I figure it might take some time. That Dain, he's a smart one, raised in the mountains and all."

"Not without me, you don't," Evie declared.

"You're a trusting soul, huh?" Elkhart said.

"How do I know you'll come back?"

"Aw, hell, come on," Elkhart said bitterly.

"Tobe's bedroll is gone." Evie cried out, running from the cabin. "He must have come back while we were out looking for the Buckletts."

"Don't surprise me none," Elkhart said. "Looks like both he and Skeets hightailed it out for different parts".

"Well," Evie muttered. "What do we do now?"

Elkhart shrugged. "Nothing lost. We'll use their disappearance to our advantage."

"What do you mean?"

"We're going into Wildwood. When those old coots hear there's a couple of killer loose in these mountains, we'll have all the help we need to find Bucklett."

"How are you going to convince them?"

"I'm not, we are," he paused. "Your brother and Skeets are gone, right? As far as we know they're dead. And we know for sure the colonel's is. Besides, they all knew Skeets; he was well liked. Skeets wanted to go back to Texas, and I figure he and Tobe are well out of the area by now. Those old trappers will believe anything after a few drinks."

*   *   *

Using the signs Dain left at the last camp Will had come across and the map he received from Don Maestas, Will had a fair idea where to start looking for more signs left by his brother. Four men didn't ride around the country without leaving some sort of trail and evidence of their passing. Assured he was heading in the right direction, Will rode easy but alert.

The effortless, ground-eating pace of the appaloosa proved to be a godsend. His wounds gave him little trouble, thanks to both the smooth gait of the horse or Juniata's gratifying care. His spirits were high, he was on the trail again, and with God's help, he would soon be with his family.

Will was approaching the area encircled on the map when he first caught the scent of wood smoke. He had seen no evidence of a fire, but the whiff was unmistakable.

He put the appaloosa over a dry stream bed and entered a stand of frost-bitten aspen. Dismounting, he removed his rifle from the boot and weaved his way up a small incline, cautiously peering into the canyon beyond.

There, in a limited clearing, surrounded by brush oak, was a small fire under a giant cottonwood tree. What little smoke the fire produced soon dissipated within the forage of the cottonwood branches. The camp was well concealed by the brush and timber around it, except from where Will now lay on his stomach. A pack mule stood munching the lush grass nearby. A large bale of furs and pelts, along with some assorted supplies sat next to the base of a nearby tree. Otherwise, the camp looked deserted.

"Ya twitch one hair an' yer innards gonna be aflyin' up the smoke hole." The voice, firm and meaningful, came from behind Will. "Ya open yer ears to me, ya savvy? Ya let go thet thar pop gun an' roll on yer backside, real slow like."

Will rolled over as he had been instructed. What he believed to be a man in fur clothing stepped out from behind a tree. The large bore Sharps rifle pointed unwaveringly at his gut not twenty feet away. The man had several years' growth of beard to match the fur coat and the coonskin cap he wore. He was about two inches over five feet with clear, beady eyes. Only his ruby red nose let it be known that, under all those pelts, there stood a man.

The old man took a few steps toward Will on the balls of his feet, alert as a caged panther. Will recoiled at the nauseating odor which preceded the gruesome sight.

"Ya get yaself sent up the flue, tryin' ta sneak up an' dee-stroy a man's privacy," the old man warned. "Whutcha want no how?"

"Just being cautious, old timer," Will declared. "I smelled your wood smoke and coffee. Figured I could share some grub, that is if you've a mind to be sociable?"

The old man squatted down into a large ball of fur. "Ya got tobaccy?"

"In my saddle bags."

"More'n apt ya wanna steal yon pelts from Ole Pincher," he said curiously.

"Pincher—that your name?"

Surely this could not be the man the don had mentioned. Still, he thought, it was an unusual name.

"Maybe tis, maybe taint," Pincher leaned over for a better look at Will. His eyes only slits, indicating possible bad eyesight. "Who ya be? I ain't seed ya 'fore."

"Name's Bucklett. My friends call me Will."

"Ya ain't no chigger to this yar coon, Bucket. Leastways, 'til I sees how ya stick floats," Pinchers paused. "Got any swallerein' whiskey?"

Will shook his head. "Just tobacco and supplies. Be glad to share. And the name is Bucklett."

Will, now curious, wondered if Pincher had met his father all those years ago. "Do you by any chance know the name Salas Bucklett from some years back?"

Pincher scratched his unkempt beard. "No Bucket 'round these har parts.' How-some-ever, I knowed a Tucky Bucket down in some Mexy high country yars back. That be ya kin?"

Will was now confused. Tucky Bucket? Salas Bucklett? Well, by some stretch of imagination, it could be and probably was, given the distinctive personage now pointing a Sharps .56 buffalo rifle at him.

"Sounds like it could have been my pa. He hailed from Kentucky originally." His eyes still on the rifle holding steady on him. "Friend, if that buffalo gun goes off, accidently or otherwise, there won't be enough left of me to fill a Bull Durham sack. I'd feel a lot better if you could point it someplace else?"

As if he suddenly realized he was being inhospitable, Pincher laughed. "Fetch ya hoss and yer tobaccy, I'm plum tarred chawin' on bark." He disappeared down the hill like a wisp of wind.

"Seen anybody back up in here lately? Like strangers?" Will asked, blowing on a tin of scalding coffee.

"Maybe yea, maybe nay," Pincher said with a squint, his mouth so full of leaf tobacco Will had a hard time understanding his words. "It 'pends whut fur ya askin'."

"My pa is being held prisoner by a gang of outlaws, and my brother's on their trail. He'll need my help, so I need to find them in a hurry. The way I figure it, they wouldn't be too far from where we're sitting right now."

"Maybe yea, maybe nay," Pincher said, said slicing the air with a stream of juice that sizzled in the fire to near drowning it out. "Be 'em reds?"

"No, not Indians. White men."

"No 'count nipple nudgers, huh?" Pincher suggested.

"Yeah, four men and a woman," Will answered, refilling his cup. "Man leading them is called Colonel Bullard. He's got two hired hands, Elkhart and Skeets. Elkhart's a killer and downright mean and vicious. Skeets, I don't know, nor do I know anything about the woman and her brother. I've never met them."

"Know Skeets, but don't know how his stick floats. But heard thet thar Bullard is a bad 'un, meanern a cut boss bull at breedin' time."

Will noticed Pincher kept glancing at the appaloosa.

"Might good horse flesh, ya got thar," Pincher observed. He also eyed Will watching him. "Hee, hee. Ye's safe, pilgrim. Ole Hannah thar' all the hoss this ole coon wants. What I seed is Maestas mark on his butt."

"You've got better eyesight than I figured. But I didn't steal him, if that's what you're thinking. Don Maestas let me have the loan of him for awhile."

"Ye and Maestas chiggered up?"

"If you're askin' if I know Don Maestas. Yeah, and he's been mighty helpful."

"Well, young'un, this ole coon's goin' be yer chigger. That's if 'n ye wanna find yer pappy."

Pincher's eyes fairly twinkled. "Thet ole coon and yourn' truly been through things thet'd melt yer dingleberries."

"Nope," Will standing up with a shake of his head. "I'll go this alone. I can't be responsible for you. Besides, that jackass won't be able to keep up, and I can't wait around on you."

Pincher turned four shades of red, puffed up like a pregnant possum, and stomped around kicking dirt every which way. "Now, lookey here, ya over-grown hunk of ham. Ain't nobody knows these har hills better 'n this ole coon. This ole coon knows ever' Injun trail in a hundred miles. I've rid 'em, walked 'em, crawled 'em. I know ever' badger hole and panther bed. Ya go in there an' yer never see the sun squat again. Ya get gin-u-wine lost. And Whutcha doin' makein' light of ole Hannah? She'll be goin' strong when thet thar mangy horse flesh you're a-straddlin' drops. Ya quit a-gapin' an' gimme a hand. This ole coon shows ya how to find them nipple nudgers."

"You know something?" Will drawled, trying too hard to stifle a laugh. "You're a regular windbag when you get started." As bad as old Pincher smelled, Will figured he would do to ride the river with, as long as he stayed upwind.

They stashed Pincher's hides and supplies of sorts in a small cave about a mile from where Will had met the cantankerous old trapper. While they covered the small treasure, Will brought Pincher up to date as to when he and Dain had met Trin in Ludlow. Pincher informed Will he had been on his way to Ludlow to do his yearly trading with Pete and Fran. There he had planned to winter out the year with his old friends, swapping yarns and drinking Pete's homemade whiskey.

When Will told Pincher what happened to Pete and Fran, the old man walked off a few paces to be by himself. The old timer remained wordless a good while after that. When the old man did start talking again, there was no shutting him up. Will learned he had lived with the Cheyenne, the Blackfeet, and the Utes. He had taken a Ute Indian for a wife who had given him a son and daughter. Their mother froze to death in a snow blizzard when she went out to collect wood, not more than fifty feet from their camp. His son and daughter now lived with the Rampart Tribe up north someplace. The last he heard he was a grandfather twice over.

Pincher was a cranky and argumentative old devil and set in his ways. But Will could sense he was a fighter and a goer, a man who would stick with his partner to his last breath. He might be meaner than a grizzly bear, but he knew he had the heart of a saint.

He kept up a running conversation of the different mountain ranges of the Rockies, the Sierras of California, and the Grand Tetons. He told Will of the mesas, plateaus, valleys, rivers, and peaks associated with those particular ranges. During the few hours Will listened to the old man, he learned more about the high country mountains and ranges than if he had traveled them himself for the last ten years.

About mid-afternoon, Pincher seemed to run out of steam. Will took advantage of the silence. "Do you know where we're going?"

"Dad-gum-come-a-tootin'. Got me an idee whur they air," Pincher retorted, stuffing more of Will's tobacco in his jaw.

Will waited, wondering if he would've been better off looking for signs than following Pincher to God only knows where.

"Har's the way I'm afigurin'," Pincher explained. "Thar be two, mayhap three, soddies whar they could be hold up. More'n likely, they be at Gomer's Gulch, but maybe not," he paused.

Will waited impatiently for him to continue. Finally he said, "Damn it, Pincher, either you make up your mind or I'm riding on."

"Now hold your water," Pincher said fretfully. "When you chase a polecat, you gotta think like one." He paused to spit. "We pass the first two and go to Gomer's Gulch by a short cut."

"I'm putting a hell of a lot of trust in you, old man," Will said irritably. "Why don't we check the others if they are closer?"

"Waste too much time. 'Sides, they not likely there. Not 'nough cover."

Will felt a little badly for his outburst. Since Pincher learned about Pete and Fran, Will knew the old timer would dog their killer to the very end.

"How far to Gomer's Gulch?"

"Two, could be three."

"Hours?"

"Hell no. Days. La Veta Pass, be thar 'morrow, if'n good weather."

Will resigned to his elder's knowledge. "Hell, let's go. Lead on."

Pincher looked skeptically at the appaloosa. "Ya might be a-totin thet thar hoss of yourn' 'fore we're done."

The sun was setting low in the west as Pincher led Will into a wide mouth canyon. As they wound their way up the canyon, the steepness of the walls increased to becoming near vertical. The deeper they went into the depth of the gorge, the darker it became. They had been in the deep narrows a good two hours when suddenly Will noticed Pincher pulled to a halt and sat staring ahead. As Will pulled up even with him, he saw why Pincher didn't proceed. He had led them into a box canyon. They would need to sprout wings or back track half a day to clear the canyon. Will's spirit drained as he saw the walls closing in around them. He wasn't thinking of his own predicament; rather his thoughts were of his father and Dain. He had failed them.

TWELVE

.

The small community of Wildwood was the inspiration of an enterprising, middle-aged prostitute by the name of Lil Sonnet. Things hadn't been all that pleasant for Lil Sonnet in Kansas City when she met a couple of trappers who staked her for the trip to Colorado, where she was told that the men outnumbered the women fifty to one. Dollar signs floated before her eyes. Upon hearing those kinds of odds, she became as fidgety as a Mexican jumping bean. So, she packed her scanty belonging, such as there were, and hot-footed it to Trinidad in the Colorado Territory. The way she saw it, this was the way the west was won.

An astute business woman, Lil obtained a tent, a mule, a few provisions, and took off for the high country. She didn't believe in waiting for her customers to come to her, she went to her customers. It took only a short time for her to find a likely location deep in the trappers' kingdom away from all competition to set up shop. From Cheyenne to Santa Fe her place of business became known as "Lil's lair." With any kind of tradable good, a man would be treated 'fair and square' at Lil's Place.

Lil soon realized the location she chose was much better than she could have hoped for. There was no local law, and therefore, no argument concerning her right to sell the land she didn't legally own. If there happened to be an unsatisfied owner or customer, she made short order of any disagreement, and she just ran them out of town—her town. She was the undisputed law of Wildwood. She ran her town with an iron hand, but a fair one. Those who unfortunately questioned her authority too harshly might soon find themselves sole owner of a two-by-six plot of their very own; donated, of course, by Lil, which was located at the edge of town for all newcomers to see.

It was these small, sloppy, marked mounds of earth Evie and Elkhart observed as they entered the muddy street of Wildwood. Most shelters were made of logs thrown slapdash together, covered with a piece of dirt canvas to keep out the rain. The canvas could easily be folded back to dry out the interior as weather permitted.

Lil's saloon was also a log structure affair, square as a box. Her quarters were also a square box-like structure, ten feet by ten feet, set in the center atop her saloon. She'd had a large window cut in each of the four walls, especially constructed to give Lil a bird's eye view of all the tents she rented out to her girls as well as other lodgers. Nothing escaped her exploring eyes.

The Two-Ace Café located directly across the street from her saloon, belonged to her former lover and two-bit gambler and sometime partner, who had only one arm. The night before the intended wedding was to take place; Lil caught him cheating at one of her card tables. Without a second thought, she promptly shot him in the arm. Gangrene set in. Still, she stood beside him as them sawed off his arm. As his arm feel off, two aces dropped from his sleeve. Although the wedding was obviously canceled, Two-Ace and Lil remained friends and business partners.

Had Elkhart been more observant he would have recognized one of the men standing on the boardwalk near the café as the half–breed they had supposedly killed in Ludlow. The half-breed spoke a few words to his companion, a smiling Mexican wearing a wide-brimmed sombrero. Both men turned their backs to the pair of riders as they stopped in front of Lil's saloon.

Lil saw all this from her upstairs' window. She knew Elkhart more by reputation than by sight. He'd been in Wildwood a few times, so she wasn't too surprised to see him again. But the woman with him bothered her somewhat. Although she was a stranger, right off Lil felt she meant trouble. Riding in with Elkhart didn't help her reputation either. Nothing escaped Lil. She'd been around the bend and back again a few times. There was a strong rumor Elkhart had a short fuse and was mighty fast and loose with his gun. She figured most of it was just more camp talk. Knowing how stories get overblown, she shrugged it off since he hadn't given her any trouble yet. Still, the tattles could have some merit since most decent men cut a wide swath around him.

These thoughts crossed Lil's mind, but her eyes stayed on Evie. She shook her head. Lil's virtues were not above reproach, and she would be the first to admit it. But the woman who held her attention gave her shudders. This woman could cause more trouble to a man, than Lil would care to imagine.

As Elkhart and Evie disappeared under the overhang of her saloon, Lil turned her attention back to the two at the café. Lil had seen the Mexican around occasionally. Pico, if she remembered his name correctly, was the Segundo for the Maestas outfit. She made it a point to know and remember everyone riding through her domain. But the big Indian was a stranger and he intrigued her. By the clothes he wore he wasn't from around this part of the country, and that worried her somewhat, not that he was an Indian, but a stranger. She'd known a lot of Indians and men of color and creed, but that didn't matter to her whatsoever. What did attract her attention and concern was his mannerisms. Or maybe it was a woman's intuition.

He carried himself with assurance, no pretense, and no wasted movement. She perceived he had seen, or had at least sensed, her watching him from behind the curtains. She felt a chill at the thought of being so vulnerable to him. Although neither his head nor his eyes had turned her way, she felt sure her privacy had been invaded. It irritated her, even angered her.

Elkhart stepped down from the saddle to find himself ankle deep in a slushy quagmire of mud and horse manure. On the split-log boardwalk he stomped some of the filth from his boots, pulled his pistol and fired in the air.

"Roust 'em out, boys," he called in a loud voice. "The drinks are on me." He fire two more shots, then continued, "Hurry it up, I ain't got all day. If you want a drink, get it now or not at all."

Riffraff, drunks, and ladies of the night of all descriptions, shapes, and sizes came scrambling from tents, makeshift. They stumbling over guy ropes and their own feet, anyway to exit, for the free drinks of rot gut whiskey. Some were dressed or were in the process of dressing, but most were not. They were stumbling along in their long johns and bare feet, while others were trying to pull on boots as they fought to be the first at the bar.

Lil slammed open her window and leaned out with her pistol in her fist. "What the devil is going on down there? Ain't nobody gonna shoot up my town 'less it's me. I'll blast the next yahoo that pulls a trigger," she demanded, her massive breasts straining to burst from their flimsy confinement.

"Nothing to concern you about, Lil" Elkhart called out roughly. "I'm going to offer the boys a little job so they can pay their whiskey bills."

Money was money, thought Lil. "Why didn't you say so to begin with?" she bellowed. She leaned out the window, catching herself to keep her balance, and emptied her revolver toward the row of tents. Yelps and screams preceded two near-naked trappers as they tumbled out into the frigid mountain air.

"Get outta 'em tents, you no good, mangy riffraff. The man's got work for you, you dang freeloaders," Lil bawled.

"Ya dang nigh took my foot off, Lil," cried a round face, breaded, fat man limping out on a bloody foot.

"Quit ya bellyaching, and get up here and see what the man wants 'fore I give you another one to match," Lil quipped.

"Men, you may not know me, but most of you knew Skeets," Elkhart began. "For you that don't know me, my name's Elkhart, and this here lady is Mrs. Plummer." Elkhart paused, smiling inwardly, noticing Evie's head down, dabbing her eyes. "Her brother has been killed. Shot down in cold blood. And so have Skeets and his partner."

"Who did it?" someone yelled above the noise of the crowd.

"Two men jumped us up at Placer Creek; they killed Skeets, who you all know, without giving him a chance," Elkhart paused, shaking his head. "Not a chance! And they ran off with all our pelts and most of our supplies. Skeets and this lady's brother took off after them, and now they're dead. Soon as I stock up on some cartridges, I'm going back looking for 'em rotten killers. Any man wants to come along; I'll do what I can to see that it'll be worth your while."

"How much?" A man called from the back.

"The lady here said she is willing to give a five hundred dollar reward to the man who finds the killers." All heads turned toward Evie; she nodded her head keeping her handkerchief to her eyes. "Also, I'll fork over twenty dollars to every man who rides with me to catch those rotten murderers."

"That Skeet was a good man. I'll go." a burly man offered.

"Me, too," another one spoke up.

"Hell, for five hundred dollars, I'll find 'em, hang 'em, and skin 'em for ya, lady."

"No," said Elkhart, holding up his hands to quiet the crowd. "We don't want 'em killed. Just find 'em, and let me turn 'em over to the law."

"Hell, that's easy. I'm the best gol-darn tracker in these here mountains ya ever seed."

"All right, meet me back here in ten minutes," Elkhart said, looking around with approval toward Evie. "Let's get 'em 'for the trail gets cold."

As most of the men thundered down the street a few minutes later, Lil noticed that neither the Indian nor the Mexican were in the group.

"Hey, Two-Ace!" Lil yelled across the empty street. "Hey, Two-Ace."

"Yeah, Lil, what'd ya want."

"What happened to the Mexican and the Indian?"

"They left."

"Figured that. Which way did they go?"

"West, toward Iron Mountain."

"Huh, now what do you make of that?" she mused softly to herself.

Skeets had always been a likeable cuss. She never heard a bad word said about him, and he seemed like a very independent individual. Not much of a trapper from what she had heard, but not the kind to tie up with the likes of Elkhart.

And that woman, Evie—if she was shedding a tear, she thought; I'll wash my hair in a full spittoon. The more she reflected on it, the more she knew Elkhart was lying through his teeth. She had never done any fur trading with him, and she never heard any of the boys say anything about him doing any trapping.

Besides, that Indian and Pico had shown more than a casual interest in what Elkhart had to say. She wondered why they were interested. No, she didn't believe Elkhart for a minute. He was up to no good. She looked toward the direction they had ridden.

"Some good men are going up the flue 'fore this is over with," she said aloud with a sigh, shaking her head.

*   *   *

Their path evidently block, Will was ready to leave the old trapper standing in his own snare, until he saw a glint in the old codger's eyes. Easing Hannah forward, he suddenly disappeared beyond a tangle of brush.

"Whutcha waitin' fur?" Pincher asked, his voice echoing down the canyon.

Behind the growth of brush, Will was amazed to find a natural corridor cut by many generations of runoff from the higher mountains.

Once through the corridor, they encountered another obstacle, a near vertical climb; Will estimated to be close to a thousand feet.

"Lead off," Will said, slightly irritated.

"It be a tad hairy," Pincher shifted his cud of tobacco. "The last few hundred feet, ya'll be a-footin' it."

Pincher assured Will he had been over Cordova Pass before, but some time back. How long ago he couldn't recall, but one time was like any other the way he saw it. The passage way became extremely narrow as they continued up the sandstone canyon. At times Will had to pull his boots from the stirrups in order to squeeze through.

The trail Pincher took, if it could be called a trail, led straight up the mountain side covered with lodge pole pine which grew almost parallel with the side of the mountain. The last hundred or so feet was covered with loose shale limestone. One slip and he would find himself at the bottom mighty fast.

At the base Pincher said, "Grab a tail and hold on; that's the best way to the top." He dismounted, took a good hold on old Hannah's tail and away they went, up the mountain. Old Hannah literally pulled the old trapper up the steep face. Will waited until Pincher was a safe distance then began zigzagging up the shear ascent. Slipping and sliding, Will finally made it to the top only to find Pincher sitting on a large boulder grinning like a corn-fed goose.

"Best we plant our taters for the night." Pincher began peeling the load off of Hannah.

The cold mountain air cut through their clothing like a sharp razor the following morning as they broke a cold camp. When Pincher told Will they should get to Placer Creek before the sun set; Will became noticeably anxious to get started. His reasoning was to get a good view of the lay of the land during the day light hours; so they pushed relentlessly, neglecting a noonday stop. Only once did they give their mounts a breather after the long climb. They still had two hours of daylight when they reached their destination.

From their vantage point, Will could only make out one corner of a log cabin built into the hillside. And it was partially hidden behind several large boulders and a thick stand of lodge pole pine. At first glance it appeared deserted. There was no indication anyone had been using the place for ages. No smoke came from the chimney, and weeds and brush grew wild around the cabin. Yet, Will's instincts told him appearance was often deceptive.

"It appears deserted, but I'm not taking any chances. There's could be someone down there," Will said, dismounting. "Cover me with that Sharps while I take a look."

On foot, Will worked his way down the sheer slope into the ravine leading up to the cabin. As he neared the structure, he lifted the throng from his pistol and jacked a shell into the chamber of his rifle. Due to Pincher's bad eyesight, he wasn't quite sure exactly how much he could depend on the old trapper shooting accurately across the gorge.

Will cautiously pushed open the door and stepped inside. Colonel Bullard's body lay where he had fallen; his life's blood soaked up by the earthen floor. He stepped over the body and approached the opening to the dugout in the far wall with uneasiness.

When he saw the hole in the roof, his spirits lift; he knew Dain had managed to get through the roof of the cave behind the cabin. He felt renewed hope. He returned outside and signaled Pincher it was okay to bring the horses down.

While waiting, Will returned for a more detailed examination of what happened in the isolated cabin. Outside again he gingerly inspected the tracks around the cabin which led him to discover a rope corral in a meadow some distance from the cabin, further up the draw. There he found Salas Bucklett's pigeon-toed old mare.

Stroking her nose affectionately, he murmured, "Don't reckon they figured you were worth taking along, old girl."

He noticed a small spring inside the confines of the corral which would provide sufficient water for the stock. Before returning to the cabin, he dished some oats from a nearby sack for the beloved beast.

"The way I'm reading the signs," Will was squatting near the outlet above the dugout. "Dain hefted Pa through this hole he'd made in the roof, then," Will looked at Pincher, "he carried Pa up through the timber," he continued, pointing toward the dense timber line. "His boot tracks are cut pretty deep; he had to have been carrying Pa. Pa was either too weak or injured or else he wouldn't have had to be carried."

"Peers they took to fightin' amongst themselves," Pincher said. "Looks to thet thar body in thar." He inclined his head toward the cabin where Bullard's body lay.

"Yeah, you're right about that," Will agreed. "Authority busted down; Elkhart's in charge now, I'd say. I'd guess—"

"Horses comin'," Pincher nudged Will to silence. "Lots of 'em."

"I don't hear anything," Will said after a moment of silence.

"Thar a-comin'. Let's get." Pincher started running toward where they had staked their horses.

With the appaloosa and the mule well hidden the two men selected a vantage point which provided an excellent view of the surrounding terrain.

As the horsemen came into view, Will counted more than two dozen riders, with Elkhart leading the pack. One of the riders appeared to sit different from the others, probable the woman, Evie Plummer. He strained his eyes for any sign of Dain or his father within the group. He was greatly relieved when he failed to spot either one on them.

"That's Elkhart out in front," Will informed Pincher. "The one I was telling you about. The lady with them must be Evie Plummer. I don't see either Pa or Dain with them, thank goodness."

"Good sign," Pincher said, raising the Sharps rifle to his shoulder. "Be no hassle a-tall ta take thet vermint booger outta his saddle."

Doubting the old man could do it with his bad eyesight, and knowing he would like to give it his best shot at the drop of a hat, Will laid his hand on the old man's shoulder. "Obliged, but they're most likely looking for Dain and Pa. Let's just keep our eyes open and see what happens."

As the couple observed the horsemen, the group split into smaller groups. Elkhart and several riders broke off from the main body and rode up the ravine toward the cabin. Pincher watched the gang, and to covered Will as he worked his way across the mountain to get better view of the cabin. The outlaws milled around the ravine and cabin in a state of utter confusion. Finally, one man broke away from the others and trotted up the ravine into the higher timber line. Pincher noticed that this person's movement was light on the balls of his feet, with head down searching for traces of a trail or tell-tell signs of a body passing.

"They've got a tracker with them," Will said, as he rejoined Pincher.

"Seed 'im. Ole Crooked Toes. Best dang Ute sign reader here 'bouts," Pincher said shifting a wad of tobacco to the other jaw.

"Pincher," Will said quietly. "I've got to draw them off before they get too close to Dain and Pa. I've got a plan I'm figuring might work, but I'm going to need your help to pull it off."

"Hells, bells, Bucket, let's get to it. I's ready fur bar. Whutcha got in mind to do?" He grinned, "Ole Pincher'll hold on to yer tobaccy fur ya."

"Pa's mare is down there, and she is well rested. I figure to sash shay down and switch mounts, letting them get a look at me on the mare," Will explained. "Not too close, mind you, just enough to make them think I'm Dain, and being on that mare they'll likely chase after me. Once I draw them away, you get onto Pa's and Dain's trail. When you find 'em, get 'em out of here, and back to the Maestas place. Can you do that?"

Pincher looked at Will like he had been insulted beyond endurance. "Gol-dang. Whutcha took me fir? Ya think I can't do anythin', huh? I gotcha this fur, ain't I?"

Feeling fully reprimanded, Will said, "Well, I figured with your eyesight and all—"

"Don'tcha fret none 'bout ole Pinch, Bucket," Pincher obviously pained at Will's doubt of his ability. "My peepers go oot, I's got a smeller, I does."

"No offense meant," Will apologized.

"Hells, bells, nairy a one took'n."

The horsemen regrouped in front of the cabin. The Ute tracker returned and rejoined the group. After a brief conversation with Elkhart, they mounted and rode out of sight up the valley.

"They'll be camping for the night soon," Will presumed aloud "and pick up the chase in the morning. I'll be ready for them at first light."

Orange rays fanned the western sky as the sun disappeared over the horizon. Appreciating the spirit of his solitude, a lone man watched the sunset, as well as the group of riders as they vanished from his view. He turned his attention back to the two men across the valley, which was hiding from the gang of riders. He walked back into the dense forest where his horse stood hipshot. He prepared a small depression in a bed of pine needles. In a matter of minutes, Booger Red was fast asleep.

THIRTEEN

Will pulled another piece of jerky from his saddlebag and leaned back against a large boulder. From his position he had a good view of the scattered campfires dotting the valley below.

Men passed back and forth causing the flames of the campfires to twinkle like the stars above. Will gave serious thought to placing a few well-placed shots among the camp in the hopes of sending a few of them packing. He could maybe scare a few of them off, cutting down the odds somewhat, but decided it would be better to stick with the plan he and Pincher worked out.

By the time they completed their plan, it was dark. Only a few stars could be seen through the increasing cloudiness, indicating a drastic change in the weather. He left Pincher and worked his way around the cabin undetected to where the mare was corralled. Leading the mare to the appaloosa, he switched the saddle to the mare, and then worked his way cautiously along the high ground parallel to Elkhart and his crowd.

Will debated with himself momentarily at the prospect of keeping the appaloosa as a second mount. Rejecting the idea he loosened the appaloosa to find his way home.

Will woke with the false dawn breaking in the east, threading through the pea soup fog that was shrouding the mountain tops. Although he could hear the men below beginning to move about and heard the rattling of cooking utensils, the scene was concealed from his view because of the heavy fog.

The intense mist sufficiently covered his movement as he repositioned himself to a more advantageous location. As he approached a small clearing, he noticed a shallow trough in the hillside caused by many untold seasons of runoff. The trough offered excellent concealment from those below. He crawled forward on his stomach until he lay behind a succession of large boulders, where he could move about without being observed.

The foggy mist lifted somewhat so that Will had a first-rate observation of the opening under the layer of cloudy mist. He had a perfect field of fire without giving away his position. They would have a very difficult time spotting his rifle fire.

Only a few of the fires had flamed into brilliance when he fired his first shot. He fired six shots in rapid succession, the first knocking a coffeepot out of a hand; the remaining shots threw red hot coals every which way. The men, those with their backsides to the fires, scattered like wild turkeys. Quickly, he switched his location and again peppered the campsite with precision.

Will had no intention of hurting or killing anyone unless forced to do so. But if he could discourage a few before the chase began, it would be a definite advantage. Some were already running toward their horses, while a few tried to return fire, shooting wildly. No shots came anywhere near Will's position.

Will smiled as he heard several horses running down the valley back toward Wildwood. Satisfied the gang would be going without breakfast and coffee, he returned where he left the mare and made his way cautiously around the mountain into the valley in view of Elkhart's camp.

He eased the mare from a grove of aspen and sat momentarily observing the scene of chaos. Calmly, he levered four quick shots toward the camp, letting them get a good look at the mare. He was too far away to be identified, but they would definitely recognize the mare. Hoping Elkhart would think Dain returned for the mare to enable him to move his father. Will's idea was that Elkhart ego would be sufficiently confident Will was dead; killed by Getchens and Walker back in Ludlow.

After firing the last shot, Will put heels to the mare. She took off like someone had slapped a hot poker to her rear. He had to haul her back some; he wanted to make sure Elkhart and his men would indeed follow. She was well rested and wanted to run, so after a couple of miles, Will let her have her head. Glancing over his shoulder, he noticed with satisfaction, they had taken the bait. So he held the mare to a walk giving her a chance to take a breather. He looked back again to see more than a dozen riders on his back trail. They're probably madder than hell, he thought. No breakfast, no coffee. When a poke is denied his coffee, he can become mighty cantankerous, that he knew from experience.

He let them close the distance somewhat before he let the mare out again. They dropped out of sight a couple of time as they rode into more broken country, so it was touch and go at times. He had only a rough idea of where he was leading them. Pincher informed him about the area and what the terrain was like south and east of a triangle formed by the Placer, the Huerfano, and the Sangre de Cristos mountain ranges. The landscape was becoming more open, the vegetation more sparse. He was going to have to be more cautious.

Reaching the crest of a high plateau, Will let the mare have a dab of water from his hat and walked her to cool her off. The ascent along the hogback ridge line had been troublesome.

However, from this height, Will could see Elkhart some three or so miles back. The gang was dragging up the rear, scattered over a half-mile behind. Only one lone horseman was working the ground a mile ahead of the gang. Must be the tracker, Will reflected.

Finally, working his way off the rugged plateau, he found he had a choice of three canyons. Pincher said nothing about a box canyon, so Will gave it little consideration as he turned toward the most likely opening afforded him.

The sky had become completely obscured with snow-threaten clouds as Will entered the mouth of the canyon. He had gone more than a mile into the canyon before he realized he made a bad choice. The walls were closing in fast and the footing became increasingly treacherous.

Gigantic, fluffy snowflakes floating lazily to cover the ground began to improve Will's mood. This improvement was short-lived as the mare began to limp badly. On inspection, Will saw she had thrown a horseshoe and her fetlock was bleeding profusely. With his horse lame, and being in an unfamiliar canyon with Elkhart closing, he felt trapper. He didn't hesitate in what action to take. Quickly, he ripped the saddle off the mare, pointed her up the canyon and gave her a whack on the rump. He grabbed up his rifle and saddle bags after stashing his saddle behind some bushes, and took off through the timber. He noticed a rocky outcropping about half-way up the mountain which he felt he could make a good stand.

*   *   *

When Juanita heard the rapid hoof beats on the hard, clay-packed earth approaching the hacienda, she immediately placed herself outside her father's office door. Her curiosity overcame any fear of being severely reprimanded if her father caught her eavesdropping.

Pico went directly to her father's office wearing a very grim expression. Some inner sense told her whatever Pico had to say would concern Will Bucklett. She knew father was up to something when Pico and Booger Red rode out early that very morning. Now she was beginning to understand why. Her father would have to make certain of the full grasp of the situation before he would make a move. She had no doubt he would keep his promise to Will, but she feared he may have waited too late to be any help to him.

Her greatest anxiety came when she noticed Pico returning without Booger Red. Concern was quickly relieved when she heard Pico tell her father that Booger Red was following the banditos. At least someone was there to assist Will. Still, she was very worried about the tall, handsome man who occupied her thoughts both day and night. If only there was something she could do. Questions flooded her mind, questions she had no answers to. She had never felt so helpless. Why was it that when she was near Will, she had a sense of well being and security? Why did she think about him so much? But most of all, why, since she had met the tall stranger, had her life been so topsy-turvy?

There was no one to talk to about her personal dilemma. Trin, the only woman her age with whom she has had contact of late, was of little help. Trin talked constantly of Will's brother Dain, whom Juanita had never met. Juanita felt in her heart, when Will returned, everything would straighten itself out. Or, God forbid, she would be more confused than she was at the present. She must find something to do, something that would help Will.

*   *   *

It was near midnight when Will left the crevice where he had taken refuge while Elkhart and his men searched the countryside for him. The snow had stopped falling leaving only a thin layer of white fluffy stuff to cover the ground. It served to his advantage that the snow started falling immediately after he relinquished the mare, covering his tracks where he had taken to the timber. Although he couldn't see them, he had heard the lead riders passing and a short time later the main body. From the sound of their voices, the cussing and grumbling above the saddle leather, the men were becoming very discouraged. Strong complaining was notably evident.

Having had sufficient rest, physical needs forced Will to leave his hideaway where he had intended to return to wait out the night. However, as he returned to his campsite, he noticed an eerie orange and reddish glow reflecting off the overhanging clouds that aroused his curiosity. He retrieved his saddlebags and with a mouth full of jerky he set off toward the illumination. Starlight filtering through the breaks in the overcast clouds gave off enough illumination so he could make his way with little difficulty.

Will found himself backtracking in the direction he been traveling when he abandoned the mare. The mouth canyon began to widen, flaring out into a fan shape field. The flat grassland was deeply cut with high-bank arroyos. The arroyos were normally dry this time of year, but extremely dangerous when torrential rains and Chinooks plagued the mountains. Will estimated the arroyos to be some twenty feet deep with sandy bottoms, and nearly thirty feet from bank to bank.

Elkhart and his gang camped in one of these arroyos in order to take advantage of the high banks for a wind breaker and to reflect some degree of warmth from their campfires. There was little vegetation to offer any degree of concealment, but by using the gullies and dry washes, Will was able to creep within earshot.

Having heard the men grumbling and griping when they passed him earlier, he gave considerable thought of producing more inconveniences which might persuade the more sulkier of the bunch that they would fare better returning to their previous lodgings.

The two men they had posted on lookout strolled indolently back and forth, one on each side of the dry channel. The main body appeared to be asleep in their blankets. Of the three campfires, the one nearest Will was dying to glowing embers. Will worked his way around to where they had strung a rope across the gully to use as a hitching rail.

Just as he started to where the horses were located, his hands touched a broken limb about three inches in diameter and eight inches long. The chunk of wood gave him an instant idea he had employed during the war.

Quickly, he began digging out one end of the limb. When he was satisfied with the depth he wanted, he began removing the slugs from cartridges, pouring the black powder into the chunk of wood. Satisfied he enough power, he packed in a bit of shavings. With a bit of saliva he rolled a mud ball and packed the shaving tightly into crude, but effective, wooden bomb.

The single picket, the one posted to watch the horses, was having a hard time keeping his eyes open. He was nodding so hard, Will was surprised he couldn't hear his neck snap. Will eased up behind the nodding-nellie and with his Arkansas pig-sticker, laid a clot alongside his head. Lowering the sleeping beauty slowly to the ground, he glanced toward the other guards. They were no longer in sight. He approached the makeshift corral cautiously.

Will cut the halter rope; know the noise of the bomb would send the horses to parts unknown. He thought about keeping one of the mounts, but on second sight, being on foot gave him the advantage of maneuverability.

Will made his way up the embankment and toward the campfires. The two guards were now nursing their coffee with their backs to Will. He eased over the embankment and gently tossed the homemade bomb underhanded toward the fire, furthest away from the sentries. The bomb landed softly, causing only a few sparks.

He had only retreated a hundred paces or so when bullets out of nowhere began buzzing around his head, followed immediately by rifle reports. Caught in the open, he flattened himself to the ground.

One of the guards was standing on the edge of an embankment preparing to fire another shot. Abruptly, his hands flew up into the air. He disappeared into the arroyo.

Taken by surprise, Will saw showers of sparks and white-hot coals fly into the air as bullets from an unseen rifleman peppered the camp fires. He must remember to thank his guardian angel. The shooting from his unknown benefactor from across the valley continued as Will began hot-footing it to safer country. Just as he reached the edge of the timberline, there came an ear-shattering explosion.

The detonation had created such a concussion that the men had to yell to one another to overcome the ringing in their ears. One of the men was yelling and pointing in Will's direction, but that did was added to the pandemonium.

The man Will had cold-cocked came wobbling up the draw. Unaware he was one of their own, those at the campsite got trigger happy and started blasting away. The poor fellow never had a chance of a snowball in hell.

Their mounts, now with no saddles on them, had broken loose from the make shift corral. The deafening sound of the blast sent them thundering for parts unknown. They would be as skittish as a prostitute at a church social for some time to come.

Will landed on his wounded shoulder. His hand came away sticky with fresh blood. The pain was becoming more intense. He realized he had to stop and care for it soon, for his pace was becoming discernibly slower as he ascended in altitude. And the higher he went he began to get lightheaded.

*   *   *

The cave was extremely cold when Dain awoke. He was shivering so badly he had difficulty starting a fire. As the flame caught and warmth began to fill the cave, he turned to his father. Satisfied Salas was resting peacefully beneath the pile of pelt and blankets, he turned to check their hideaway.

He eased out of the mouth of the cavern. Being careful not to outline himself, he kept low behind some brush oak, surveying the countryside. Their position lay just below the summit of the mountain, with enough height to see most of the valley floor below. Mentally, he noted likely areas of fields of fire and spots which could afford him good concealment.

Dain returned to his father and considered waking him. Deciding to let him rest a while longer, Dain adjusted the blankets around his father's shoulders. Instantly, Salas gave a sharp cry of pain. Dain drew back the blankets to reveal a badly swollen leg.

Gently Dain cut away the leather buckskin covering his legs. The sudden release of the leather allowed the reddened flesh to expand beyond its original size. The skin was an unnatural purplish color. From the offensive odor, Dain knew instantly his father was suffering from blood poisoning. Gangrene had set in; he had seen it before, there was no mistake.

Somehow, it was impossible to say from the discoloration of the enlarged area, if he had been wounded and had not mentioned it to Dain. Dain felt a sense of regretful guilt for not examining his father more closely for further injuries. It appeared to be a deep flesh wound, and not having been treated, it had gotten badly infected. It was readily apparent he needed immediate medical attention by an experienced physician.

A doctor had to be brought here for his father. Moving him was completely out of the question. But where in all this wildness would he be able to find a doctor? There wasn't even a town, settlement, or community Dain knew of, or even heard of for that matter.

Then Dain remembered someone had left the cabin the first night after their arrival. He must have been going to some kind of settlement. He racked his brain trying to recall if anyone had mentioned a name of a town or settlement of any kind. Yes, Wildwood was the name. But where? Which direction would it be? If it was within riding distance, then it was surely within walking distance. Maybe they had a doctor there, or at the very least knew how to get a hold of one. Whatever the outcome, he wasn't helping his father just standing here.

Varied amounts of snow had fallen on and off the past two days. Dain hurriedly fashioned a pair of snowshoes, just in case the need arose. He would stay to the high ground, hoping to catch sight of some kind of living soul as he surveyed the horizon. The sun was well past its zenith and had broken through the overcast, when at last Dain at caught sight of a sliver of a smoke column beyond a low ridge off to his right. Elated, he increases his stumbling pace.

A number of wooden crosses dotted the landscape on Dain's right as he entered the muddy street of Wildwood. Although, he was trembling with both relief and exhaustion, he didn't stop until he stepped onto the porch of Lil's saloon. Only a couple of rib-caged pony's stood hip-shot at the hitching rail. Viewing the deserted street, Dain's hopes took a sudden downturn. Where was everybody?

Dain pushed open the double batwing doors. Two men dressed in ragged range garb, which had seen better days, sat hugging the single potbelly stove in the center of the room. A half-empty whiskey bottle sat on the floor at their feet. Socks that were more holes than socks were draped on the back of a nearby chair. Fowl-smelling steam from the drying socks gave off a stench which was near as unbearable as it could possibly be.

A third man, the bartender, stood with his backside to the red glowing heat with a dead cigar clamped between his massive lips.

Tobacco stains streaked his once white shirt and the apron around his abundant waist.

"I'm looking for a doctor," Dain said politely.

"Who's asking?" sneered the overblown bartender.

"Me."

"Who's me?"

Dain's patience ebbed quickly. "Is there a doctor around here or not?" His voice became firm and unfriendly.

"Naw, ain't no doctor around here. Least ways, not a real doctor. You sick or somethin'?" The bearded speaker shifted in his chair as he reached to scratch the toe jam from between his toes.

"My pa is down. And he needs a doctor badly."

"What happen? He got gun shot or what?" his companion inquired.

"Blood poisoning. He could lose a leg or worse."

"Ya had a run-in with somebody maybe?" Toe Jam smiled.

Ignoring the question, Dain tried another approach. "Maybe you could tell me where abouts I would be able to find a doctor, or perhaps I could get the use a horse?"

"Maybe you be one of them that murdered Skeets?" Greed for the reward money showed in Toe Jam's eyes. "He was a good friend of ours. We done a sight of riding the trails together and shared many a can of beans. Boys, I think the reward money just walked in the door."

Dain stood stunned, uncomprehending the turn of events. "Look friend, I don't know what the hell you're talking about. I'm just looking to help my pa who happens to be in a bad way. I've got no time to waste."

"Sure, I'd be in a hurry too if I had half of Colorado on my tail," his companion stated.

The conversation was taking a very angry, unpleasant tone. Any other time, Dain would have welcomed a knock-down, drag-out fight, but now was neither the time nor the place. Getting help for his father was imperative, and getting people all upset and their noses out of joint was not the way to go about it. However fruitless it might prove to be, he felt he had to try and head off any immediate confrontation with these men. Time was running out for Salas. For all he knew his father could be dead now.

"Look, I only met Skeets once, and then he did me a good turn. I've got no cause to bring any harm to him. When I last saw him he was alive and kicking."

"You're a lying," Toe-Jam insisted.

"Yeah," his partner agreed. "We done heard how you folks bushwhacked him and his partners and took off with all their trappings.

Well, you elegant talking dude, we're just going to hold you out back in the smokehouse 'til Elkhart and the boys get back so we can collect our reward." His hand streaked to his holstered pistol, but he never cleared leather. Suddenly, he was sitting on air for there was nothing beneath him. Dain's foot had sent his chair flying across the room. Before he hit the floor, Toe Jam was staring into the business end of Dain's rifle, his eyes the size of tea cups.

The bartender had backed up to the end of the plank bar, waving his hands in the air, "Not me. Not me. I didn't do anything." He wanted no part of the quick-acting stranger.

"Put it away, stranger. There'll be no more gun play in my place." Dain turned to face the open end of a double barrel shotgun.

"Joe, help Slim up off the floor. And get them stinking socks off my chairs. Whew! I never! Don't ya'll ever scrub the crud off yourselves?" Lil's demanding, booming voice shook the walls.

"But, Lil," whimpered Slim, "this here fella is one of them that murdered Skeets and his partner, and stole their pelts. Why—"

"Aw, shut up, you skinny drink of water," Lil interrupted angrily. "Can't you see further than the nose on your dirty face? Elkhart ain't done any trapping, and you know it. He wouldn't know what work was if it slid in bed beside him. And Skeets, he's got more sense in his little toe than the lot of you wooden blockheads. He's no deader than the man in the moon. He's probably half way back to Texas by now. That's where you ought to be if 'n any of you had enough sense to poor piss outta ya boots, which you ain't. Now get outta my sight, at least out of smelling range, the both of you. Get out." She glanced at Dain. "Well, what are you staring at? Ain't you ever seen a lady before? Or do they grow them where you come from?"

"Not quite like you, ma'am."

"Should I take that as a compliment or just slap your face?"

"A compliment for sure, ma'am. My apologies for the little ruckus. The boys were getting a bit carried away with their assumptions."

"Were they? It didn't look like you were worried about it too very much." Lil grinned looking at Dain.

"Why, yes, ma'am. I came in here right polite, like, asking if there was a doctor about, and they up and accused me of murdering one of their friends. Besides, I don't take kindly being called a lair. If Skeet is dead, it surely is none of my doing. Fact is I did meet him a short while back and he seemed like a decent sort, just maybe running with the wrong crowd."

"I sure hope you're right about that. What is it you needing a doctor for. Maybe I can help."

Dain explained briefly about his father's condition and his immediate need became apparent to Lil.

"Mike," Lil turned to the overweight bartender. "Throw a saddle on my horse and dust your tail over to Seedway and fetch Doc Thruman and bring him to . . . . Where do you have your pa?"

After all he had been through, Dain was reluctant to tell anyone about the cave, but he had little choose. He needed help; he had to take the chance.

"Come on, come on," Lil said testily. "Look, I don't give a hoot-n-hanner about your pa; he's no kin of mine. But if you want our help you've got to trust someone. Besides, I don't care for Elkhart running roughshod over this county. It cuts into my business." She paused. "You know, your pa could be dead already. There's no time to waste if'n he's got gangrene, I can tell you that much."

Reluctantly, Dain gave the location as best he knew.

"I know just about where you're talking about," Mike said, stripping away his apron. "But you stay on the lookout for me and the doc."

Lil started for the door; over her shoulder, she yelled, "Grab a couple of bottles of whiskey, better have a slug for yourself. It looks like you could use it. I'll run across the street and get Two-Ace. He's had some experience at doctoring, even if it was horses. I'll have him saddle a couple of horses for us."

"Make it three. I'm afoot."

"In this stuff! Hell, you'd better make that two slugs."

"Make it a whole damn bottle," Dain muttered. Lil hadn't heard; she was already out the door.

As they rode steadily on, Dain told Lil and Two-Ace what he knew of Colonel Bullard and his pack of cutthroats and the events as he had knowledge if. He also related what had happened in Ludlow. He had no idea what happened to Will and Booger Red. They both may be dead, but deep down inside he had doubts. He had faith that both men were certainly able to handle any situation they might encounter. They had always been quite capable of taking care of themselves. When Lil told Dain what took place in Wildwood, Dain felt sure the Indian had been Booger Red.

"That would be Booger Red, but the Mexican I don't know," Dain said.

Dain started thinking, if Booger Red was alive, then where was Will? As soon as he saw to his father, he would make for the Maestas hacienda in the hopes of getting a lead on Will's and Booger Red's location.

Up ahead a group of riders broke from the timber line and was riding hell bound toward them. Dain shifted his rifle to lie across his saddle, hammer cocked.

FOURTEEN

Eyes red and scratchy from the lack of sleep, Will checked his wounded shoulder he had packed with snow to help coagulate the flow of blood. Even though it still ached like hell, he was relieved to note the bleeding had stopped. Still he felt physically drained. Somewhere, he couldn't remember where, he had lost his saddle bags; now he had no food whatsoever.

After the little foray down in the arroyo, he kept to the high ground as much as possible. His main objective was to put as much distance as possible between him and the pack of wolves. He tried to recall if this was the second or third day since he left the Maestas ranch. He kept getting confused, his mind wandering. He needed rest, lots of rest. He was cold, hungry, and just downright perplexed. Where were Dain and his father? Where was Booger Red? At first he thought the lone rifleman last night was Booger Red. If it was why hadn't he shown himself afterwards? Whoever it was sure saved his bacon with that impossible shot. As improbable as it seemed, it had to be Booger Red. He felt quite positive of that.

Will checked the cartridges for his rifle, and revolver and started descending the mountain. He needed to find food, by getting down the mountain where there were wild berries and other edibles grew. Energy was of the utmost importance, he had to get some edible food.

He'd neither seen nor heard anything of the Elkhart crowd after the incident at the arroyo. He was beginning to think they might have turned back, but on second thought he couldn't take the chance. Did they come to the conclusion they had been duped and returned to Dain's trail? He just didn't know; he was too tired to think.

Will almost missed the broken sucker limb. He inspected the break closely. The break was fresh, only caused a short while ago. He was not alone on the mountain. Then he noticed the tracks of a shod horse. About every hundred yards or so, the rider had stopped and sat a spell, listening and watching, never dismounting or staying in one place too long. Whoever the rider was, he was extremely cautious and careful. Shortly after reading the signs left by the individual, Will was convinced the man was one to be reckoned with. The man was probably one of the trackers Elkhart had employed. Will knew he was fortunate the man hadn't found him.

Knowing Elkhart was still on his trail brought mixed emotions. He was relieved to know they hadn't pulled off his trail and returned to try and located Dain and his father; on the other hand, he was getting mighty tired of being chased and shot at. He'd had enough. Now it was time for the hunted to become the hunter.

Will whirled around at the sound of pounding hooves. Two horsemen, appearing out of nowhere, were bearing down on him with determination on their faces, and grinning from ear to ear in anticipation of reward money. It was obvious their intention was to ride him down like a dog, but Will stood his ground, his mind made up. He would run no more.

As they closed the gap, Will stood firm. Judging correctly, he gripped his rifle by the barrel, and backed off a step to the side. He brought the tube of the cold, hardened steel across the nose of the horse nearest him. The animal squealed like a riled cougar, reared up, and came down on his haunches. The man in the saddle was thrown in the path of the following rider, who tried at the last second to rein away from the fallen man. As he veered away, his horse took him under a low hanging limb. By the sound of the thud of his head colliding with the tree, Will knew without a doubt the unfortunate man was dead before he hit the ground. The other chap was up on his knees trying frantically to claw for his holster.

"Hold it," Will cautioned.

The man froze; stark terror showed on his face as he stared into the business end of the .44 Winchester.

"Where's Elkhart?" Will ask harshly.

The man glanced at his partner's bashed-in head. "I don't— know," he stammered.

Will thumbed back the hammer.

"Sweet mother of God, mister. I'd shorely tell you if I knowed," he said, shaking his head, fiercely. "They're scattered all over these hills looking for ya."

"But where is Elkhart? He's the one I want. I'll not ask you again."

"Please, mister," he pleaded, nodding toward his dead partner. "Me and him was just a-getting' ready to pull out 'fore we spied ya through these timbers. Honest, we was."

The man was too scared to be lying; he was shaking like a leaf in the wind. "You go find Elkhart, you hear. You hear me good. You tell him I've got the gold he wants. If he wants it bad enough to die for it, come and get it. Just him. No one else. Tell him it's just him and me, just like in Marysville. You got that? Just like in Marysville."

"Yeah, I've got it," he said with relief. "Just like in Marysville."

"How many men does Elkhart have left with him?"

"No more than seven, maybe eight, one less now," he paused. "I'm getting the hell out of here."

"Deliver my message to Elkhart first," Will warned, "or I'll look you up when this is over."

More color drained from his already pale face. "Yeah, I'll tell him. I shorely will. You can depend on me."

"Okay, get."

The man looked around for his horse which was nowhere in sight. Will knew what he was thinking. "You don't need your horse. Start walking 'fore I take your boots."

The man took a few steps and then turned toward Will, "Man, I don't know who you are or where you came from. But you shore played holy-hell with that Wildwood bunch. They're all madder than all hell for what you done to 'em. You get out of this alive, you'd best stay shy of 'em if you want to keep on living."

"Friend," Will said impassively, "you can pass the word around in Wildwood and anywhere else you want. As soon as I'm finished with Elkhart, I'm coming to Wildwood and hunt out every man that hired on with him. You tell them this, Will Bucklett pays his debts. And I figure I owe them." Will paused, letting his words sink in. "I mean every word of it, mister. Now you find Elkhart, my patience is about worn out."

As soon as Elkhart got the word, Will knew he'd be coming, but not alone. He wasn't to be trusted. He didn't know how much time he had before the hired gunman found Elkhart and gave him the message. As for now, he had to find a place to make a stand.

Will began working his way around the side of the mountain seeking the best place for cover and concealment. He encountered a shear drop of five hundred feet or more to the river below as he came out of the grove of golden-leaf aspen. He changed directions to follow the river. It was no time to be caught with his back to the deep ravine. It was an obstacle he couldn't afford.

He smelled the odor of burning pine the instant he saw the three men hunkered down around a campfire in a small clearing. One of the men spotted him before he had a chance to duck back into the timber. The man yelled and grabbed for his pistol. Will leveled his rifle and fired as the others pulled iron. Will's first shot went wild. He began backtracking as bullets started kicking dirt around him. His next shot caught a tall lanky man in the chest. His screams echoed off the canyon walls as he fell from the cliff. The other two ran for cover. One of the two, a large bearded man, ran head-on into a tree as a bullet knocked his leg from under him.

Will felt the sting of hot lead sear his right thigh? If it didn't break the skin, it burnt like all Hades.

They had him backed to the edge of the deep gorge. He turned to run along the rim. His foot slipped on a loose stone. He tumbled headlong into empty space. He remembered hitting some thick brush, which help to break his fall. Still, he plunged again and again. Then he was rolling, unable to stop. Suddenly, everything went black. He struggled to open his eyes, but the engulfing darkness overcame him.

*   *   *

Juanita sat on her bed in total dejection. If she just had something to do to pass the time, she thought. Normal activities lacked any importance. She hadn't been away from the ranch house since their return from Ludlow. Maybe she needed to get away for awhile. Perhaps a long ride, she thought. She would let the cold, raw wind blow away the disconcerting thoughts running around in her head.

Hurriedly, she changed into her riding clothes and rushed toward the corral. She climbed to the top rail and watched as the vaquero cut out her a horse. A sight that met her eyes almost caused her to lose her balance. The appaloosa Will had ridden away was among those in the corral. The appaloosa was obviously favoring one of her hooves. Will had obviously released the lame mare. He would now be on foot and in need of help. She must tell her father right away.

No, on second thought, she knew he would not let her accompany any search party. If she told him about the lame mare, he would demand she remain at the Hacienda. He would want to know if Will was in some danger. What should she do? What if something bad had happened to her Will and she did nothing? She would never forgive herself. She caught herself. What did she mean, "her Will"? He was a stranger. She hardly knew the man. Still, she thought, she must tell her father or he would be very angry with her. What would her father do? Would he quickly assemble the men, and ride to assist Will and the others? Or would he wait another day as he had promised? No, she would not tell him! One of the vaqueros would tell him soon enough. She would take the chance that her father would not act immediately. But she felt she had to take action, so it would be up to her to help Will. She quickly found Jose and quickly told him she wanted to go for a ride. Though reluctant, he agreed accompany her, after some serious arm twisting. At her father's insistence, one of the vaqueros was to always accompany her when she went riding.

Juanita went quickly to the kitchen. Pleased to find no one around, she tossed some food into a sack, filled a canteen with water, and located a few medical supplies, just in case.

Jose had the horses saddled and was ready to ride. She was please to see he hadn't forgotten the rifles. "We will eat?" Jose smiled, eyeing the sack of food Juanita tied onto the saddle horn.

"Si, Jose," she returned his grin. "It is a nice day for a picnic on the bluffs. Don't you agree? The ride will make us hungry." She felt slightly deceitful for not telling Jose the whole truth about the reason for her ride. But under the circumstances, she felt she had no alternative. If she had revealed her real purpose for the ride, he would have surely refused to accompany her.

"Si, Senorita," Jose said. "I am hungry already. So I will get us to the bluffs pronto."

They rode until they were out of sight of the ranch building, when Juanita suddenly pulled to a halt.

"What is wrong, Senorita?"

"It is getting cold, Jose. I think I should have brought my heavy coat."

"The sun will be on the bluffs as always. It will be very warm there." He started forward.

"No, Papa will be very angry if I become sick." She glanced knowingly at Jose.

"But, Senorita—"

"Do not worry, Jose. I will sit here on this warm rock until you return." She smiled. "Now go, pronto. Marie will know which coat I need. Go, I am getting hungry also."

When Jose returned, Juanita had disappeared. Perplexed, he scanned the countryside, but Juanita was nowhere in sight. Her tracks leading away from the rock where he had left her, pointed toward their intended destination.

Fear for her safety began to set in. He was becoming very upset and angry his senorita would put herself in such danger riding out alone. She was his responsibility. Don Maestas would be extremely angry with him. He became agitated.

At the bluffs, where they would normally picnic, there was no sight of Juanita or that she had ever been there. Should he spend more time looking for her, or return and confess his ineptness to the don? He was damned if he did, and damned if he didn't.

Juanita had never been in this part of the country before. She had left familiar country some time ago, riding cautiously. She had made a mental picture in her mind as she watched through the crack in the door as Pico and her father encircled this part of the map as the most likely area Salas would be held prisoner. She wasn't afraid, but she had sense enough to be careful.

She was beginning to think she had gotten herself lost when she spotted a riderless horse grazing leisurely in a lush meadow. She saw immediately why the animal had been abandoned; it was missing a shoe and limping badly. As she approached the animal, she recognized the saddle as one belonging to the Maestas brand, but not the horse. It was the same saddle Will had placed on the appaloosa mare. Now why was the saddle Will used on the appaloosa mare now on an unfamiliar and strange horse? The only answer she could think of was that Will was either in real danger or possibly dead. It was too far back to the ranch to alert her father. She could only hope and pray she wasn't too late to be of some help.

She thought it would be easy to back tracking the animal with the missing shoe. She soon learned she was not a tracker. Still, she saw no alternative except to do what little she could to locate Will. That's what she had in mind to do anyway, wasn't it?

Juanita followed the tracks of the mare until she lost the trail as she crossed a rocky creek bed. Her attention was on trying to spot where the mare had entered the small stream when she heard gunfire. The sound of the shooting echoing up and down the gorge caused her to question which direction she should take.

*　　*　　*

"Easy," Lil cautioned Dain, as he brought his rifle up. They stopped waiting for Elkhart's rag-tail remnants of deserter to close the gap. She continued. "They're a harmless bunch, mostly drifter, and no-accounts, with little gall and even less guts." She nodded toward Peabody. "What happened to ya'll Peabody? Looks to me like you boys met up with some wildcats." Lil laughed.

"Ain't no cause to make fun, Lil," countered Peabody.

Some of the men wore bloody bandages, while others appeared as if they had been rolling around in a bed of red hot campfire coals. Several were covered with blisters, as seen through their burnt and ragged clothing.

"Aw, some jasper jumped us whilst we was having our coffee, throwing hot coals and boiling coffee over everybody that was hunkered down around the fires. Hoppy, back there, got him a busted knee, and Ross got hit in the arm. The rest of us is burnt somethin' fierce. We were riding over to Doc's to get patched up some." He paused and nodded toward Dain. "Who's this gent? Ain't never seed him 'fore."

Lil ignored his question. "You boys don't have the good sense God gives a billy goat. You go off doing that no-account Elkhart's dirty work, now look at you." She paused. "We don't have time to sit and palaver. You all get on to my place and don't drink all my liquor. You do and I'll skin you all alive, now get."

As they started to turn away, Dain ask, "Where is Elkhart?"

Peabody frowned, looking at Lil. "Who is this fellow, anyway?"

"Brother to the one that made you all eat dirt, and he is about twice as bad," Lil answered.

All eyes turned toward Dain, who held his rifle at the ready.

"Don't worry, fella," Peabody said. "We know when we've had enough. Elkhart was up the gorge near Chimney Rock taking out after you brother. And he's mad enough to kill him when he catches him."

After the men were out of earshot, Dain said, "They were lucky."

"What do you mean?" Two-Ace asked.

"Will is the best shot going, bar none," Dain explained. "Especially with a rifle. You can bet your bottom dollar if he wanted to hit someone, they'd be pushing up daisies, no doubt about it. But my guess is that he was just trying to pull them off my backside so I could take care of Pa."

Lil shook her head. "If that's the case then he could be in big trouble. That Elkhart is a mean one. And some of those he hired in Wildwood would cut their own mother's throat for a shot of rotgut whiskey. And that she-devil with him ain't much better."

Dain's heart jumped in his throat when he noticed fresh tracks leading toward the cave where he had left his father. Although they were tracks of an unshod horse, it made little difference; they led straight to the hideout.

Lil and Two-Ace shook their heads, indicating they had no knowledge who the mule belonged to which stood outside the mouth of the cave. Cautiously, Dain entered the cave alone, his revolver drawn, hammer cocked. Huddled over his father's prone figure was what appeared to be a huge ball of fur.

"You make a move, mister, and you'll be shaking hands with Lucifer," Dain promised. "Raise 'em high."

"Well, tarnation, young fella. I could've picked you off way down yonder comin' up the trail," Pincher said, not turning or paying attention to Dain threats. Reaching for a pan of water, he continued in a commanding voice. "This har yer pa, ain't it? Why don't yer quit a-gapin' and give me a hand 'fore he goes up the smoke hole."

Dain glanced over the old man's shoulder. His father's swollen leg was wrapped in a thick layer of tobacco under a cloth soaked in hot boiling water.

"You a doctor?" Lil asked.

"Maybe am, maybe ain't."

"That's the most gol-durn thing I ever did see," Two-Ace exclaimed, looking at the mass of tobacco on Salas Bucklett's leg.

"Yeah, maybe, but it will sure draw the poison out," Lil explained.

Pincher squinted at Dain. "Ya got some tobaccy? I done squirted my last chaw."

                         *   *   *

Evie was in such a foul mood, the men kept their distance. None of them quite knew how to cope with a woman who had such a mean disposition. Had she been a man, not one of them would have taken the misery she was dishing out without a fight. She and Elkhart had a knock-down, drag-out altercation the night before and again this morning. None of which didn't seemed to help matters in the least. The fight this morning came just after Sam died. Sam's screams as he had plummeted to the floor of the gorge had unnerved them all.

Although, Elkhart really didn't give a damn about Sam, when one of the men had given him Will's message, he went absolutely wild. Evie's fury boiled forth.

"You colossal dolt!" Evie screamed. "You're so pathetic; you make me sick to my stomach. You've been following the wrong man all this time. Your stupidity is overshadowed only by your nerve that you could do better than John Bullard." She became more incensed as her tirade continued. "John was ten times the man you are in every way. Bucklett has led you on a wild goose chase, come near blowing us all the kingdom come, and we're damn near freezing to death. All the food is gone and all you can say is, 'don't worry.' If John was here—"

"Well, he ain't!" Elkhart shouted, interrupting her. "Just shut the hell up. I don't want to hear about John or anyone else. If you don't like the way I'm running things, then go ahead, turn tail and run. Ain't anybody going to stop you."

"You'd like that, wouldn't you," she yelled. "You'd have the gold all to yourself. Well, over my dead body, you will."

"That can be arranged easily enough," he threatened. "But for your information, maybe there ain't no gold. I never believed there was. Didn't you hear what the man said? The man wants me to come to him. Do you think for one minute he would risk losing any gold if he had it? Naw, not Bucklett. It's personal now. Just him and me. And that's just the way I want it."

"You're stupid. You know that, Elkhart? Just down and out, flat stupid."

The back of Elkhart's hand contacting with Evie's jaw had the sound of a gunshot. Evie found herself looking up into the gray overcast sky, eyes watering, and her cheek on fire.

"Maybe, ma'am, just maybe," he ground out between gritted teeth. "But I'm a hell of a lot smarter than that ridiculous tyrant you started out with. From now on you keep your mouth shut and do as you're told."

"You lay another hand on me again and I'll kill you," Evie blurted out angrily.

Elkhart took another slug of coffee and threw the cup on the ground. He walked over to the men squatting by the fire. "Schultz, take Boone and Sloan, get up there and keep a sharp lookout."

"There's already three men up there," Sloan said.

"Don't bet on it," Elkhart stated. "You don't know Bucklett like I do. And remember, all bets are off. I want him dead, you hear? Dead! You all heard what Ham said. Bucklett said he had the gold, didn't he. Well, get rid of Bucklett, and it's an even split right down to the last man. You men want your split, then get Bucklett!" Elkhart couldn't believe these men were actually gullible enough to believe him. The only pay they would receive would be a bullet in the back once they served their purpose.

"I'm going up this side of the gorge," he told them. "When I've flushed him out in the open, you know what to do."

FIFTEEN

Something was burning nearby. Subconsciously, Will knew he smelled wood smoke and could hear the crackling of pine knots on an open flame. Confusion replaced unconsciousness as he attempted to get his eyelids to respond.

It was terribly cold, yet somehow he felt hot flushes, a burning sensation on his back. Wave after wave of nausea diminished gradually as his brain began to slowly come into focus. He tried to remember where he was and what had happened.

Gingerly, he attempted movement. Twinges of needle-sharp pain flared throughout his body. Though the prickly aches seemed to help clear his mind somewhat, he hesitated to force any further movement for fear of increasing the uncomfortable thorn pricks.

Ever so slowly, as if coming out of a foggy mist, his mind began waver. He remembers crashing into bushes, limbs, bounding into nothingness. The fog cleared as he recalled the rolling— never ending rolling—and then everything went blank. He vaguely recalled there had been three men huddled around a blazing campfire. Then there was gunfire; someone screamed as he plummeted off the ledge to the valley floor below.

It was ever so cold.

He opened his eyes to the dancing reflection of flames on the earthen wall he was facing. An icy breeze touched his face, yet he could feel warmth on his back through the blanket that covered him.

A blanket?

Will's first thought was that he was now Elkhart's prisoner. But that deliberation was absolutely ridiculous, Elkhart want him dead, so why the blanket. In utter confusion, he strained to roll over to face the fire, expecting to see some mighty unfriendly features, definitely lacking in cordial welcome.

The cloaked figure bending over feeding the fire appeared to be that of a woman. He blinked with perplexity; the figure was somewhat familiar in the gloomy light, with the flame's reddish-orange on long silky hair.

Will brushed his eyes with the back of his hand in order to try to clear his blurred vision.

Juanita?

Was he dreaming?

It was impossible, he thought. He was either hallucinating or becoming delusional. But when he caught the faint scent of lilacs, he knew she was for real. Glancing around he realized they were alone.

Juanita turned toward Will. "It is good you are awake. I was having great concern. How do you feel, Senor?"

"Like I've had a run-in with a grizzly and lost—to tell you the truth," Will managed, between swollen lips. "I thought you were going to call me Will?"

"Si, Senor," She offered him a canteen of water. "You must be very thirsty?"

"How did you get here? Where are we?"

Will struggled laboriously to raise himself to lean against the wall of the cave.

"I will tell you later. Here you must eat this soup," she offered. "It will make you feel better and give you strength."

Painfully, favoring his shoulder, he found a somewhat comfortable position and accepted the tin cup of steaming broth. She noticed the grimace of his expression. "You must let me look at your shoulder," she frowned. "It is bleeding."

It was an ugly looking wound. Juanita soaked the bloody dried cloth which had adhered to the wound so she could remove the old bandage. She began cleaning it with a water and herb mixture she heated in another tin cup. Her touch was light and delicate. Meticulously, she washed and removed all foreign matter from the old arrow injury. She then applied a salve which smelled so bad it took Will's breathe away. It took all the willpower he could muster to not complain about the odor, to say nothing of the pain. She turned away and tore some material from the tail of her shirt, which she used to bound his wound more securely.

Juanita wasn't one to waste words or time. She knew what had to be done and got right to it with no squawking, no nagging, and no complaining. Though accustomed to wealth, she was a very resourceful woman when the need arose.

"Where are we?" Will asked again.

"We are in the Santana Bluffs, between Bandito Cone and the Greenhorn Mountains. We are many miles from the hacienda." She paused for a moment. "Those bad men are still very close by."

"What are you doing here? How come you are here?" Will frowned. "And how in the world did you find me, and—?"

"Jose and I were out riding and I . . . we were separated. I came upon a strange horse that had the saddle you used to ride the appaloosa. I followed her tracks, then I heard the shooting. When I rode over to investigate, I saw two men standing on the edge of the bluffs looking down into it. I was curious what they were doing. I waited until they left and then I started searching; then I found you. I almost missed you. You were under some very heavy brush and covered with snow, which had followed you down the side of the cliff. If it wasn't for the snow you dislodged as you went into the ravine I would never have found you.

"We will be safe here for only a little time. The bad men who hunt you? They are no very far away. Two times I heard their voices." Juanita hesitated before asking, "Did you find you brother and papa, Senor Will?"

Will shook his head and gave a weary sigh. He put his hand on his holster. It was empty.

Juanita noticed his movement. "Your rifle is here. But the pistol, I did not find. I am sorry."

The breech of the Winchester had been damaged during the fall. It would serve little purpose except as a club. Without going into all the redundant details, Will related what transpired between Pincher and himself and his hope for Pincher's success.

"I have faith in this Pincher of whom you speak. I think you do not have to worry about you papa and brother," Juanita assured him.

Will could not say why, but Juanita's reassuring words lightened the burden he was carrying since he, Dain and Booger Red left Arkansas.

"What you do now?" Juanita's expression showed faith in his abilities.

"I'm going to find Elkhart," Will spoke matter-of-factly, "and put a stop to all this once and for all."

"Yes, I think you maybe right, but you are hurt," Juanita said. "My father—" She paused. "There must be some other way. You will be killed. They are many."

"Elkhart won't quit until he finds my father and Dain. He's not the kind to quit," Will assured her. "I've got to stop him before anyone else dies."

Will heard the noticeable intake of her breathe, her expression one of dread and fear.

"Look, Juanita, he . . . they have to be stopped. They've been responsible for too many deaths already. There is no other way."

"You would shoot a woman?" she asked in disbelief.

"I don't know," he answered honestly. "I never have, but if it comes to her or one of mine . . . well, we'll just have to wait and see. It may not be necessary.

"When will you go?"

"The sooner, the better," he answered. "Do you have a pistol?"

"Si," She reached into her saddlebags and produced a Colt .45 and a hand-full of cartridges. "But you must eat and rest before you go. I have prepared food."

Will was black and blue with bruises from head to toe. Suffering through the initial shock, he began testing his movements with more difficulty than he anticipated. Luckily, he sustained no broken bones, although his arm felt totally useless from the many punishments his shoulder had received. Juanita's heart went out to him as she watched him struggle not to show the agony he was suffering in his maneuverings.

"You said they were close by," he said, returning to the fire. "How far would you say their camp is?"

"I do not know of the camp," Juanita said slowly. "I only heard voices coming for the canyon where I found you. I believe they were looking for you. After darkness, I heard them no more."

"Do you know the way back to the ranch?"

"Only that it is south," she said.

"At dawn, you light a shuck back to the ranch," Will ordered. "And don't stop until you get there. Understand? Your father will have men out looking for you."

Juanita's facial expression was one of shear stubbornness. Will had more sense than to say so, but he had seen that same unyielding, headstrong look in many a mule's eyes. He knew instantly he was in for a battle.

In a no-nonsense tone, Juanita said, "I will stay with you. I did not ride to help you, only to run away. The only way I will return to the hacienda is if you take me there, and stay with me until you recover. What will be, will be, Senor Will Bucklett."

Not being able to grasp the meaning of her words puzzled him. When he finally realized what she had just said, he stared at her in awe. He was speechless. The beating of his heart increased to send a pounding to his temples. A lump developed in his throat that was hard to swallow. His felt an embarrassing blush. His face was hot with humiliation. He was a kid who just got caught with his hand in the cookie jar.

Will, being a man of the outdoors began to feel closed in. Not because of the confinement of the cave, but Juanita's statement literally rocked him to his inner core. Why was he feeling so elated? He wants more than anything, to take her in his arms. But because of his present state of utter confusion, he was afraid he would bungle the attempt or destroy the wonderful feeling of intoxication.

Red-faced, Will turned toward the mouth of the cave. Juanita's horse, standing hipshot, turned as he approached. He wrapped his arms around the animal's neck. On the eastern horizon, a faint pink radiance promised a new day. He returned to the fire keeping his eyes to himself. He didn't trust his emotions. He squatted and sipped his coffee from the hot rim of a tin cup in an attempt to organize his thoughts. The fresh air had always seemed to clear his thinking. But this morning his brain refused to function properly. He was having trouble organizing his way of thinking in an orderly, prospective manner. Expressing his true thoughts, in certain special situations, could possibly be more devastating than not speaking at all. Horses he understood, but women—?

Will forgot the time as he sat thinking about the present and what the future might hold. As the surrounding mountain took shape with the coming dawn, he became aware it was time to send Juanita back to her father's ranch, even if he had to knock her out and tie her no her horse. If she came to any harm he could not live with himself. He could not bear the thought of that.

With his cup long since empty, he rose to return to the cave. Three shots rang out almost simultaneously. The side of his face was peppered by a ricochet striking the wall entrance to the cave. It felt like a thousand bee stings. A second of shots made a wicked, deadly sound as they buried themselves into Juanita's horse.

Fearing the worse when she heard the shooting, Juanita ran head-on into Will. They went sprawling to the floor.

Disengaging himself, he said, "Looks as if you will be staying after all. They just killed you pony." Pulling Juanita back into the cave to safety, he continued. "Now they have us trapped like a couple of gophers."

"They will kill us?" she held her head high, looking into his eyes.

"Not Likely. Not if I've got anything to say about it." He put his hand on her shoulder. "Elkhart wants me. That's all he cares about right now. I think I might be able to make a deal with him. That is, if I can talk to him before I get shot first. Not to worry, I'll get you out of here."

"No, you will not die because of me," Juanita said bluntly. "There has to be another way."

"Not unless we can dig our way through this mountain. And I see very little chance of that." Will said gently, "Juanita, you're just going to have to trust me."

Will walked to the mouth of the cave. He cupped his hand to his mouth. "Hey, you out there," Will yelled. "Ask Elkhart if he wants to make a deal; if he does, I'm ready to trade."

*   *   *

"Hey boss, the man wants to talk to you," Boone yelled down to the camp.

"What does he want?"

"He says he has a deal to offer you," Boone replied.

"I still can't believe you followed the wrong man," Evie said, walking back and forth, slapping the quirt against her leg.

Elkhart hitched up his gun belt and turned away. "Stop your damn nagging, will you?"

"Where are you going?"

"The man wants to talk, so we talk," Elkhart said sarcastically.

"Hey, Bucklett, you up there in the cave," Elkhart called through cupped hands. "You want to talk? So talk."

"Want to make a deal," Will's voice echoed from inside the cave.

"Ha, you ain't in no position to make a deal, Bucklett," Elkhart laughed uproariously. "You sound mighty weak. You sick or somethin'?"

"There's a lady in here," Will shouted. "She's got no part in this. Give her a horse and let her ride out . . . ." Will's voice faded.

Elkhart looked questioningly at Evie. She shook her head vigorously, bewildered.

Elkhart cackled, "You take the cake, Bucklett. How'd you get a lady in such a predicament, anyway?"

"Let her ride out, Elkhart. Then it's just you and me. That's what you want, isn't it?" Will called.

"No. Oh no," Elkhart cried out. "You tell me where the gold is. And then, if you're telling me the truth. You can both ride out, safe and sound."

"Elkhart, you know as well as I that there never was any gold," Will assured him.

"He's lying!" Evie cried out. Her hopes and dreams were long in dying.

"Not Bucklett," Elkhart said knowingly. "I know that man. There's not a lying bone in his body."

"You're such a damn fool," she shouted, turning away. Where had her life gone wrong, she wondered. If there was no gold as John promised, then there is nothing worth living for. No trip to Europe, no rebuilding the plantation. All her dreams were shattered. Shot to hell, as they say. What did she have left? Nothing. What could she do at her age? Work as a common person? Preposterous. There had to be gold.

"Boone," Elkhart grinned, "come with me."

As Evie watched, Elkhart pulled a half dozen dynamite sticks from his saddlebags and said a few words to Boone. Boone jumped on his horse and took off up the mountain with the explosives.

"How about it, Elkhart?" Will called down.

"Hold your water, Bucklett. I have to talk it over with my partner." He needed to stall for time to let Boone get in position.

"Can he be trusted?" Juanita asked.

"No further than I can throw this mountain," Will assured her. "He's up to something; stalling for time most likely. He's never asked anyone permission for anything."

Will picked up Juanita's rifle. After checking the loads, he belly crawled to the mouth of the cave. He studied the far wall of the ravine looking, for a likely spot for a sniper. He selected a clump of bushes among some boulders. A probable spot, he thought. He fired a series of shots into the undergrowth. Someone cried out, cursing wildly. His action drew immediate return fire from both his left and right flanks. Hot lead began ricocheting off the nearby rocks into the cave. Will dove headlong back into the cavern out of harm's way.

Juanita cried out suddenly.

Fearing Juanita had been hit, Will shouted, "Are you alright?"

"I think so." She was holding her ankle. "I believe I turned my ankle when I fell to the ground."

Will assisted her back into the depths of the cave. Pain crossed her expression as she applied weight on her foot. As Will cautiously lowered her to the floor, she said, "I don't think it's very serious, just turned."

After checking her ankle to make sure it wasn't a serious sprain, Will said, "I hate to leave you alone, but I have to try to find us a way out of here."

"There is no other way to go," Juanita murmured.

"I believe there is," Will said hopefully. "Earlier I noticed the flames fluttered slightly, not much; but enough to indicate a breath of fresh air from the back of the cave. You should be okay here until I can get help. I don't think they'll try to rush you, but I'll leave the rifle here. If you hear anything, just fire a shot out there. That should hold them back.

Elkhart's playing for time and it's time we don't have with what little food and water we have."

"Will?"

"Yeah?"

"I'm sorry I've caused you so many problems," she said apologetically. "Be careful."

"None of this is any of your doing," he assured her. "No need to apologize. You were trying to help. I'm the one who should be apologizing. I'll be back for you soon, don't worry," He tried to sound convincing. "Just trust me."

"I do."

He would like to put his arms around her, but could not bring himself to act in such a forward manner. Had he realized that at that moment, Juanita would have given anything for him to embrace her, he might have done so. But with a huge lump in his throat and his heart pounding wildly, he only nodded and reluctantly turned away.

Will began descending the depth of the cave's cavity with a small torch he fashioned. With every step he advanced, the way became smaller and smaller; soon he was crawling on his hands and knees. Breathing was becoming more difficult, causing him to doubt if he imagined the flicking flames.

Maybe he was on a fool's errand, he wondered. Leaving Juanita alone was not what he wanted to do, but did he have another choice? Still, he saw no other way. He pushed all doubts aside hoping and praying he was doing the right thing. Their very lives depended on his decision.

His tiny torch flickered, almost going completely out. For a moment he thought he had lost it, and then a heartbeat later it flamed up again. Was it his imagination or had he felt a slight brush of air on the back of his hand? Nature plays funny tricks on a man's mind in the dark depths of the earth. He thought he heard a sound like muffled gunfire. He stopped to listen. Nothing. No sound of any sort—eerie silence. Deathly silence. Murky blackness playing tricks on his mind, he thought He forced himself to calm down and began creeping forward again.

He tried to put his mind on other things. Had Pincher found Dain and his father? Were they safe at the Maestas ranch? If he could just get to Elkhart he could put a stop to all this.

Once again the close confines of the walls began to unnerve him, pushing all rationale from his brain. Would the cavity become a coffin in which he and Juanita would be buried alive? The memory of the solitary confinement he suffered in the union prison come flowing forward to his consciousness. He began to sweat and shudder as old haunts floated forth. He must back out and return to Juanita. They would fight and die together.

Suddenly, something soft touched his cheek, the air cooler.

A far off rumble of thunder echoed within the closeness of the walls around him. He felt the ground sway beneath him. Then he realized it wasn't thunder, but a cave-in.

Juanita! She was alone at the other end of the cave. Fear for Juanita gripped his senses as he scrambled back through the tunnel. Choking dust filled his lungs as he fought his way along the obscure route to the opposite side of the mountain.

Coughing, choking, he stumbled into the chamber where he had left her. It was in complete darkness. The campfire had been smothered out completely.

"Juanita," Will called frantically.

No answer.

"Juanita," he called again. The only response he received was his own heart beating wildly.

He struck a match. The dust was so thick he could hardly see the massive hill of rock and rubble blocking the entrance. Somehow Elkhart had caused the mountain to come down on them, sealing their doom.

Fearing the worse, Will's heart stuck in his throat when he saw something white at the base of the enormous mound of earth and rock. Juanita had been wearing a white scarf around her neck.

SIXTEEN

From his position, Booger Red was not able to see the entrance to the cave where Will and Juanita were cornered, nor did he have a view of Elkhart's camp. He was watching the three men hidden in the brushes and rocky outcropping along the mountain finger which jutted out where he was located. He knew Will was somewhere on or hidden in the bluffs across the gorge, but he hadn't been able to pinpoint his position until he heard the conversation between Will and Elkhart. He was relieved to know that Will and the Mexican girl were alive.

He had been only a mile or so down the valley, attempting to pick up Will's tracks, when he heard the rattling exchange of gunfire earlier.

As Booger Red maneuvered to better his position behind one of the men, he shook his head in wonder. Will was harder to trail than a panther. Twice he had been on the verge of hailing Will since the night at the arroyo, but Will had suddenly disappeared like a puff of smoke. He smiled to himself as he recalled the night Will had tossed the explosives into the enemy's campfire.

Booger Red shimmied over a flat boulder to look down on a man in a faded, red shirt. Quick as a cat Red dropped down twenty feet behind the man. A few brisk steps and the barrel of his rifle did the job. The fellow never knew what suddenly put him in a deep sleep. Red was able to catch the man's rifle in time to eliminate any noise. Another faction of a second later it would have rattled off down the shale of limestone below, setting off an avalanche of slate.

Red had just begun making his way toward the remaining two men when they spotted him. He was momentarily stunned as he was forced to dive headlong behind some huge boulders for protection. He landed on his damaged ribcage, knocking the breath out of him. He was raising himself to his knees when he was knocked backward against the mountain by a terrific blast. In awe Red watched the bluffs across the gorge disintegrate. A great portion of the mountain started cascading into the depth of the chasm. The entrance of the cave, where he suspected Will and the Mexican girl had taken refuge, disappeared instantly.

As the rumbling diminished, the remaining two gunmen stood up with a shout. Booger Red calmly placed his rifle to his shoulder and started firing. The two men followed the landside of rock and rubble.

*   *   *

Will swiftly applied a match to a twist of twigs for better lighting. His heart sank as he noticed the ugly twist of her right leg. Quickly, he moved the debris off Juanita. But, thank God, she was breathing. She apparently tried to make a run for safety, but with the bad ankle, she was unable to escape the avalanche. Luckily, she had gotten as far as she had. A step shorter and she would have been buried under tons of rock.

Filled with rage, Will picked her up and carried her away from the pile of debris. He made a vow to himself that those responsible would pay dearly.

He found the undamaged canteen and held it to her lips. Her eyes fluttered open, releasing glistening tears down her dusty cheeks.

"It hurts," she moaned softly. She was trying hard to hold back the tears, but the pain was too great. Her eyes seemed to ask Will to remove the hurt.

"I know, girl. Just rest easy. I'll get you out of here," he promised, holding down a gut-wrenching storm grumbling deep inside. He made a silent oath to himself: he would find Elkhart and literally tear him apart with his bare hand, along with that damn she-devil, Evie.

"I'll have to set this leg. It's broken," Will informed her sadly.

"Yes," was all she could manage to say.

"It's not going to be easy." He lifted her head and gave her another drink.

He knew he would have to hurry; there was no time to waste. The lack of air was beginning to slow the flame of the small fire he built.

Will saw no other way. Her eyes were closed. Now was as good a time as any. He gritted his teeth and let her have a solid punch to the jaw. She was out like a light.

Wasting neither time nor motion, he set the broken leg and applied splints, using the damaged rifle and strips from the blanket.

They were trapped with no possible means of escape. And no one knew of their predicament except Elkhart and his henchmen; and as far as they were concerned he and Juanita were dead.

It would be impossible for Will to dig through the mass of rubble before they suffocated. There was no alternative except to go through the mountain as he had attempted previously. There was no other way. It was not in him to admit defeat.

Will carried Juanita as far as possible toward the rear of the cave. He then wrapped Juanita in what remained of the blanket and began dragging her.

He wondered how far it was to where he had turned back. Had it been a hundred yards? Two hundred yards? He had no way of knowing, just knew he had to do what he could. There was no turning back this time. It didn't occur to Will to question whether or not he felt air on the back of his hand on his previous trip.

Suddenly, in the darkness of the tunnel, his head butted against a stone wall. His first thought was that he was lost. Was there another tunnel that he found on his first excursion and had somehow missed this one? He tried to calm the panic building up inside him. He had to stay composed, unruffled, and in control. He forced himself to think above his beating heart, as he ran his hand over the face of the wall. He could feel no air as he had before. Had he pulled Juanita as well as himself into their deathbed? In the closeness of the tunnel there was no room to turn around. Even if he could, there was no way to squeeze by Juanita. To turn back, where would they go? He couldn't back out as before. He must stay relaxed, he must believe. Think. Think.

No! Of course he wouldn't be feeling air. There would be no air flow with the tunnel being blocked at the other end by the explosion. The pressure would be equal throughout the passage way. Almost frantically, he begins searching the face of the wall again. He compelled his hand to move slowly, sensitively.

There was a small crack in the face of the wall. He began working slowly at first, with increasing speed he tore at the earth and stone. He soon had an opening large enough for his arm. He reached through and could not feel any obstruction on the other side. He could see a dim shaft of light through the hole. He became so elated he tore frantically at the opening.

He soon had Juanita lying comfortably on the floor of a large sun-drenched carven on the far side of the mountain. Finally they were safe. But he knew he had to remove the threat of Elkhart and his desperados before he could move Juanita from the safety of their present location. He must deal with Elkhart first.

Satisfying himself she was resting easy, he placed what little jerky they had left within her reach. He shook the canteen; only a small amount of water remained. He set that also within her reach. After checking the revolver, he climbed through the hole which allowed the sunlight to enter the large chamber. Somehow, somewhere, he must get a horse to enable him to get Juanita back to safety of the ranch. By the time he reached the hole the throbbing in his wounded shoulder was excruciating. On top of that he was hungry, tired, and damn mad.

As the abyss of the chasm and the bluffs came into view, he moved more cautiously. The landslide had spilled tons of rock and earth all the way down to the floor of the ravine. The ledge where Will had stood and the mouth of the cave were no longer recognizable. He shuddered at the thought of Juanita's and his destiny had he not found a way out through the mountain.

He stopped and listened intently for a sound which would give him an idea to the direction of Elkhart's camp. All he could hear was the music of the sweet sound of the wind playing through the tall pine.

Moving lower to get a better view beyond a grove of aspen, he came upon a clearing made by a previous landslide of shale limestone. It apparently happened ages ago. The slide reached from the top of the mountain to the very bottom of the chasm. He saw no other way except to make a beeline for the other side. It would be very treacherous footing—one misstep and it would be Katie-bar-the-door. About midway across, a gigantic tree had been uprooted by the slide. Its upturned enormous root cluster left a crater some ten feet in diameter and nearly as many feet deep.

He started limping toward the cavity as fast as his battered legs would carry him. He found he was holding his breath, expecting a bullet every step. As he neared the depression he began to wonder if Elkhart and his bunch had pulled out. The nearer to the hollow he got the more confident he became. But suddenly a bee zipped by his head, brushing the hairs on his head. Realizing it wasn't bee, but a bullet, Will took two long strides, and threw his body in the hole left by the uprooted tree. Bullets pounded the rim of the hole as he attempted to burrow down out of sight.

"It's Bucklett!" someone yelled. "How the hell did he get out of there?" The fellow was answered with a string a curses.

He heard angry voices coming from down below. He was about to make a run for higher ground, but then shouts came from both sides of him. They had him surrounded; they had him on all sides. He had no way out. He stood about as much chance as an icicle tossed in the fire of a blazing belly-stove.

Will wasn't thinking of himself as much as he was Juanita. He failed her. Back there in the cave with a broken leg and no one to help her. No one knew where she was or if she was alive, except him. More than likely folks would assume she had been buried beneath the rubble of the dynamite blast. He had to make someone listen, not for himself, but for Juanita's sake. Otherwise, it wasn't likely she would ever be found. Maybe years from now some wandering soul might stumble across the crack in the hillside and discover what was left of her bones.

"Elkhart!" Will roared. He had to tell them about Juanita, whatever the cost.

His only answer was a hailstorm of lead.

Will saw no hope for the situation he had gotten them into. He had been such a fool leaving Juanita alone, and now each of them would die alone. But if I'm going to die, he promised himself, I'll not die alone. Elkhart is going with me.

"I think I winged him," someone shouted.

"Me, too," said another.

"Elkhart," Will called. "You chicken-livered tub of bile, you want me? Come and get me. It's just you and me."

He lay stone still, listening. He was thinking of Juanita and the life they could have had together. But dreams, at times, have a way of dying a swift and final death.

He heard the crunch of footsteps nearby. Hopefully, it was Elkhart, but he wasn't alone. He counted two others. That was okay too, as long as Elkhart was one of the three. It was Elkhart he wanted.

They approached cautiously, tightening the circle around him. Memories of his childhood floated before his eyes. Visions of pleasant scenes flashed in a panoramic view, shutting out the present world, but only momentarily.

He wiped the dirt from his eyes with the back of his hand. Through half closed lids a red bearded face came into focus above the rim of his future grave. Elkhart? No! Will had only to move the cocked revolver a fraction of an inch. The pistol bucked contentedly in his fist. The red bushy face disappeared with a .45 slug in the middle of his forehead.

Will stood, his worn out and battered body drawstring tight. He was anticipating the impact of, and expecting, a driving rain of hot lead. He had only five cartridges remaining, but he intended to make good use of them. There was no doubt he was going to take some of Elkhart's men with him. He just wanted one of them left for Elkhart. He would not die until he saw Elkhart's blood flowing into the dirt. It would end here. Now! Somehow he always knew it would come to this. The memories of Sergeant Elkhart's criminal and devilish abuse of prisoners flashed through his sub consciousness.

There was a lot he hadn't gotten to do in his short life and a lot he dreamed of doing. But apparently it didn't seem to be written in the Master's Book upstairs.

He heard a rifle shot, then another. Heavy gunfire broke out as someone returned fire. The shooting was off to the left, and they weren't shooting toward him.

He saw a bright orange flash out of the corner of his eye. Simultaneously, the impact of a bullet spun him around, throwing him back against the wall of his death trap.

With his back to the wall, Will stared into the murderous face of Elkhart. Elkhart stood on the edge of the opening, leg apart, grinning wolfishly, and his smoking pistol level with Will's chest.

Somewhere a man screamed in agony.

Elkhart's grin was replaced by a vicious sneer.

Instantly, the pistols in both men's fists recoiled, belching lead and smoke. Will didn't feel or hear the ugly thud as lead from Elkhart's .45 slammed into his body. He eyes were only on Elkhart as he squeezes the trigger again, and again, and again . . . . With a nightmare of eeriness, a blanket of darkness enveloped Will into its waiting arms.

*   *   *

Will regained consciousness in a brilliant sun-drenched room. Juanita sat beside his bed, white lace covering her bowed head. She raised he head. Their eyes locked in understanding. Smiling broadly, she rose on crutches and snuffed out the lone candle burning near the Madonna.

"This candle will never burn again," she said softly. "But I shall keep it always."

Will followed her gaze. In a bed across the room lay Salas Bucklett, resting comfortably.

"Juan says he is too tough to die," she informed him. "He says your father will only die after he has seen many of his grandchildren."

Will could not speak; he had a lump in his throat too large to swallow. Juanita smiled gently in understanding as she noticed moisture sparkling in his eyes.

"Yes, this Elkhart is dead." She enlightened him, "but the woman, Evie? No one found her. All the other bad men are dead or have been taken to Trinidad by the authorities.

"Booger Red followed your tracks back to the cave where you left me. And your brother, you can see him yourself." She turned toward the window. Through the lace curtain window, he watched Dain and Trin stroll, side by side, carrying on an animated conversation. As Trin took Dain's hand, Juanita found Will's.

Will's eyes blurred as he gave a silent prayer of thanksgiving. Everything he loved was here. He was home with his dreams intact and within his grasp.

ABOUT THE AUTHOR

Jim Workman was born during the Great Depression of the 1930s'. He served in the U. S. Army Artillery during the Korean Conflict and as a meteorologist during two tours in Vietnam. He was the middle child of nine children of an impoverished family, who some folks referred to as migrant workers. He well remembers the hard times, and the unforgiving existence of the Dust Bowl days. The author was willingly obligated to help provide for the welfare of the family. Before entering the service he worked at several summer and fall jobs, from the paper mills of Northern Louisiana to the cotton fields of the Pecos River Valley of Mew Mexico. While working as a farm laborer and ranch hand along the Red River Valley of North Texas and Southwestern Oklahoma, he had the distinctive privilege of a first-hand education of the western frontier and the men who helped build this great land. He has attempted to re-tell and relate bits of the historical knowledge he has experienced, and common-sense wisdom as told to him by the ranchers, cowboys, laborers, and just common, everyday folks of those unforgettable years from his childhood through "Bucklett's Pursuit."

Jim now resides in Fort Smith, Arkansas, an area rich in historical accounts of the dangers of the wild and rugged American frontier. An avid fan and reader of western lore, both fiction and non-fiction, he (at the urging of his "hardest critic," his wife) continues to write his stories of America's west.

CPSIA information can be obtained
at www.ICGtesting.com
Printed in the USA
LVHW091536080820
662690LV00001B/62